# Copper and Stone

stories

Bethany Snyder

This is a work of fiction.
Names, characters, businesses, places, events, and incidents
are either the products of the author's imagination or
used in a fictitious manner. Any resemblance to actual persons,
living or dead, or actual events is purely coincidental.

ISBN-13: 978-1516992614
ISBN-10: 151699261X

Printed in the United States of America

"I Spied" first appeared in *Petrichor Machine* in April 2013.
"Underneath" first appeared in *Kindred* in Summer 2013.
"The Stone Wife" first appeared in *Geek Force Five #6* in September 2014.
"Through the Storm" received the Charles McCorkle Hauser Prize
from the Chautauqua Literary Arts Friends in August 2015.
"Jackpot" first appeared in *Lost Coast Review* in Winter 2015.
"Three Times Fast" first appeared in *Geek Force Five 2015* in September 2015.
"Jam" first appeared in *Commonthought Magazine* in 2014.

bethanysnyder.com

# Contents

For Geraldine Turner,
a promise kept.

# I Spied

It's cold and snowy and windy, but we have snow suits, moon boots, big fat vinyl mittens and hats with fuzzy ear flaps. So Mrs. Spencer says okay, we can go out, but only for an hour, and then back inside for hot chocolate, maybe some marshmallows if there's any left in the cupboard. She always gives us crumbly graham crackers smeared with vanilla frosting from a plastic can.

Me and Gary and Jeremy and Gary's little brother L.S. go single file down the icy sidewalk from the kitchen door, across the gravel driveway in front of the barn where Mrs. Spencer parks her station wagon with the Disney World sticker on the bumper, and along the path between the pine trees that leads right into the cemetery that, before I met Gary, I didn't even know was there. In the summer, Dad would drive the car fast down Second Milo Road to the next town so we could get vegetables from the farmer's market, and I maybe saw there was a house on the corner, but I sure didn't see an old cemetery right there by the road. Even from the upstairs window in the bathroom that Gary and L.S. share, you can't see the cemetery because of the barn roof and the pine trees around it, which are even taller than the barn.

The cemetery goes all the way from Second Milo Road where Gary lives, back a country block to Old Bath Road. It's new out back there, with frosty flowers and cracked urns that people put there on Memorial Day and the Fourth of July the summer before. But up front near Second Milo Road and Gary's house is the old part, with crumbly stones and some graves that are fallen right over on their fronts so you don't know who's buried there unless you lift the graves up, which Gary dares me to do but I never do.

The cemetery goes right up to the edge of Second Milo Road, which is a busy road with tractor trailers on it all times of the day and night, which Mrs. Spencer always complains about. And right next to the road, almost in the stones on the shoulder, is the weirdest grave of all: Goonrad Shadik's. None of us guys believed Gary that the dead man's name was Goonrad, so one night when me and Jeremy were sleeping over, Gary took his dad's flashlight and we snuck out to look. If Mrs. Spencer and Gary's dad knew, they would have been so mad, because to see the front of the grave you have to stand right in the road shoulder.

The worst part isn't Goonrad Shadik's name, which is kind of weird but mostly stupid, but the creepy skeleton face with no eyes right above his name. Gary's big sister Bridget said it was an angel face, but that's even worse, an angel with no eyes. After seeing that face with the flashlight shining on it, I had no-eye angel nightmares for a week and slept with the nightlight on I hadn't used since I was a baby. But I didn't tell anybody and shut it off first thing in the morning.

The old part of the cemetery is the best part to play in, Hide and Seek and Cops and Robbers and Cowboys and Indians. But we almost always end up playing Spies, because Gary likes Spies and it's his house. Spies is a pretty dumb game, and Jeremy thinks so too. When you play Cops and Robbers or Cowboys and Indians there's lots of running around and yelling which I like, but with Spies the whole point is to be really still and quiet so you don't get caught.

Everybody stays super still and doesn't talk until someone can't stand it one second more and they get up and sneak around and try to shoot the other players before they get shot. Gary thought Spies up and I think he made it up because he doesn't like to run around. Gary's pretty fat.

It's easier to play Spies in the summer when you can wear camouflage pants that make you invisible laying on the grass or under the lilac bushes. As long as you don't wear a yellow shirt or orange, which I did the first time and got shot by Jeremy right away. After that, Dad bought me a camouflage t-shirt.

But there's so much snow now we had two days off school, and everybody's snowsuits are blue or red. Gary, trying to sneak around behind a wide black gravestone, looks like a big fat blueberry on top of vanilla ice cream. Jeremy's hat is white but has purple and yellow stripes so I can see his head easy from where he crouches by the fence that has sharp wires sticking out that can tear a hole in your jeans if you try to crawl over.

The trick with Spies is to pick the best starting spot, and the best spot is behind this one really tall grave near the pine trees so there's lots of cover. You just put your back to the trees and then you can poke your head around the side of the monument and see a guy sneaking up on you. But Gary's little brother L.S. is already hiding there.

L.S. isn't Gary's little brother's real name, it's Lawrence. Gary told his mom that L.S. just means Lawrence Spencer, but when Mrs. Spencer wasn't listening he told Jeremy and me it means Little S-h-i-t. I'm not allowed to say that word, and neither is Gary but he says it sometimes when he's mad.

L.S. has his mittens pressed up on the side of the tall grave like he's going to use it to launch himself off and tackle anybody who gets too close. L.S. never understands Spies, that you're supposed to be super quiet and not move until you see the eye whites of your enemies. He just wants to jump on someone and knock them to the ground and then hit them on the head usually. He's only five.

I find an okay spot behind a row of graves where the stones are close together, right in front of the steep hill that goes down to where Mrs. Spencer has her garden. I lay down on my stomach with my head to the side so most of my earflap keeps the snow off my cheek. I turn a little so I can pull my knees up so my boots aren't showing, and then I close my eyes. It's easier to hear someone coming if you close your eyes, since then your ears hear better. And when someone crunches on the snow, you can pop up and shout, "Pshuuuu!" which is the sound a spy laser makes when you hit your enemy and the only noise you are supposed to make when playing Spies.

Gary whistles, long and really loud, and that means the game is started. I hear L.S. sliding his boots around on the snow because he never has any patience, even at the beginning of the game. When you're only five it's way better to play Cowboys and Indians or something else when you can run around a lot and yell. That is a thing me and L.S. have in common, even though I'm almost three years older than him.

From where Gary went to hide over by the dead lilac bushes I can hear him breathing heavy. I take a quick peek between the grave stones and see the back of Jeremy's blue snow suit as he moves behind a grave just two rows over from me.

Now the trick of the game is to see who can be still and quiet the longest. When L.S. is playing, he always gives up first, but the rest of us can stay still for a really long time. Last summer we played Spies after fried chicken dinner which is Gary's dad's specialty, and we played for so long I fell asleep and Jeremy and Gary went inside for root beer floats and forgot about me. I woke up with fireflies buzzing around my head and ran inside really fast and acted like it was no big deal. But it was really creepy to wake up alone in a cemetery in the dark, and I never want to do that again.

After a little while, maybe only five minutes, I hear someone walking on the snow. It sounds like it's Jeremy, who likes Gary more than me and who almost never gets sick of Spies and starts going after his enemies right away—that makes Gary mad, but it is really cold so I'm sort of glad Jeremy is doing it. But I don't want to get caught, either, which I will get if I stay where I am.

I squeeze my eyes shut, tuck my arms against my sides and roll backwards, down the hill toward Mrs. Spencer's garden. I spin around really fast and hope I won't puke Spaghettios and milk, which we had for lunch. And then I bump into the trunks of the pine trees and I open my eyes. I stay very still. My snowsuit isn't blue or red, it's brown, so maybe Jeremy won't see me. I'm kind of tucked up under the branches. There aren't any shadows to hide me, because the sun isn't out and the sky is white as the snow.

Jeremy comes running fast around the row of close-together graves in a crouch. He sees me, but in Spies you aren't allowed to shout anything until you are close enough for your laser gun to hit your enemy, which is very close according to Gary. Jeremy slips in the snow and he falls on his butt, but he slaps a hand over his mouth so he doesn't yell out loud. I could get up right now and race up the hill and shoot Jeremy, but then I see Gary army-crawling up behind Jeremy, and Jeremy doesn't know it, so I just watch while Gary points his mitten at the back of Jeremy's head and shouts, "Pshuuu!"

Jeremy kicks at the snow and says a curse word, loud.

I move back a little more into the trees, really quiet, and pine needles poke me in my head through my hat. Jeremy is talking to Gary, but I can't hear what he's saying. Jeremy looks mad, or else his face is just red because of how cold it is. He stomps away and walks over to Goonrad Shadik and sits down on top of the grave.

No one knows who Goonrad Shadik is or was, or when he lived or died, since the numbers on the grave are all worn away. Gary likes to tell L.S. that if he tattles on him to their mom and dad, then Goonrad Shadik will come get him in his sleep. Jeremy should not be sitting on Goonrad Shadik's grave. If Mr. and Mrs. Spencer see him, everyone will get in trouble, not just Jeremy. But Gary's dad works on Saturdays, and Mrs. Spencer is inside with Bridget making dinner, so Jeremy hops right up and sits there like he's allowed to do it every day.

Meantime Gary is standing at the top of the hill looking at Jeremy, and I bet he wants to tell him to get off the grave, but if he says something he breaks his own Spies rules and then I win the game. Gary hates to lose more than anyone I know. The best idea is to just charge right up the hill at Gary. So I get to one knee as much as I can under the branches and put my hands down on either side of my foot. I'm going to pounce out of the trees and race up the hill before Gary knows what's happening. I never get Gary at Spies, nobody every does. Gary always wins, but not this time. It's so cold we can probably talk him into giving up after one game and go in for hot chocolate and graham crackers.

I count under my breath three, two, one, and jump out from under the branches, but my foot slips in the pine needles and I go right back down on my chest, knocking the wind out of me and saying "oof" before I can stop myself.

Gary turns and sees me. He flings himself right down on his butt and slides down the hill. Half way down he points his mitten at me, and I know Gary's thumb is cocked back and his finger is pointing to make a laser gun. "Pshuuu!"

I'm already out of the game because I made a noise, but anyway Gary shouts and I'm dead for sure.

Gary slides to a stop right next to me, and then we both look up because we hear L.S. shout, "I got you, I got you!" L.S. always forgets to be quiet. He jumps over three rows of graves like the high school kids doing hurdles on the track, and then he bends over and puts his head down. He's going to head butt Jeremy off Goonrad Shadik's grave.

Gary and me grab at each other as we run up the hill, slipping. I pull my mittens off with my teeth so I can get a better grip on the snow, and I am running to grab L.S. but I am never going to grab him in time. Gary is huffing and puffing and halfway down the hill still and I am the only hope.

Jeremy puts his legs straight out to stop L.S. and kick him backwards, but L.S. turns to the side and hits him and they both go shooting over the top of the grave and out onto the shoulder of the road, and the slush and ice slide them right out into the road.

\*\*\*

Gary's sister Bridget gives me hot chocolate even though I want to see the ambulance and the fire trucks instead. Bridget doesn't make me graham crackers with frosting because she doesn't know Mrs. Spencer gives them to us for treats, and she doesn't even try to find any leftover marshmallows. Gary is up in his room and won't come out and his dad bangs on the door but Gary doesn't answer. Bridget and me sit in the kitchen and don't talk and watch the yellow lights in the side yard from the tow truck out on the road. The tractor trailer is on its side in front of the graveyard and they had to call three ambulances, one for Jeremy and one for L.S., and one for the truck driver who was mostly shook up but not hurt, I heard Gary's dad tell Bridget. I listened hard because then he was whispering, and he said Jeremy hasn't woken up yet, and he might not ever. And L.S. might lose his foot, or maybe his leg. His whole leg! I don't know what L.S.

will look like with only one leg. Then Gary's dad started to cry and he told Bridget he would call her from the hospital and he left.

Later Bridget makes me put my snowsuit back on because my dad is going to be there soon to pick me up, and I ask her if I can wait outside. She is on the phone with her mom at the hospital and she says okay, but stay on the porch, don't go near the cemetery, but I don't want to anyway. I walk out to the driveway, though, and hop from one boot to the other because it's really cold and my feet are already freezing to the ground. Dad pulls up in the truck and I get in and shut the door. He asks me if I'm okay and he puts his hand on my shoulder for a minute. Then he goes to make a big U-turn to drive back to town. I look over and even though it's almost dark I can see Goonrad Shadik's grave. I close my eyes tight and stay very still, the best Spies I've ever played, if I'm super still and quiet, Goonrad Shadik's angel smile won't get me. I think about marshmallows and vanilla frosting and I don't move or make a sound the whole ride home.

# Underneath

In the late winter of 1932, Edward Sorensen stopped speaking. While it is true that he witnessed the death of his brother that day, which was February 6, a Saturday, and that he himself suffered the loss of the baby toe on his left foot, it was widely considered to be a self-imposed silence, and not a result of the trauma, both physical and emotional, that he experienced that afternoon.

The silence was more than simply not speaking. Edward didn't sigh, or grunt, or make any sort of noise that would have been useful in his family's attempts at communication. He was as silent as the death that had taken Thomas under the water.

The closest Edward came to speaking, before that night in July when he started up again, was on the second of May, what should have been his brother's fifteenth birthday, when his parents decided to donate Thomas's things to the Salvation Army, including the baseball that Edward wanted for himself. He did end up with the ball; when his parents were occupied with packing the boxes into the car, Edward slipped the ball under his sweatshirt and carried it up to his room, where it lived under his bed for almost a year and was eventually lost when the family moved to Chubb Hollow Road.

"Yes," was the first thing Edward said when he decided to talk again. The cousins from Connecticut were visiting, and while the men threw horseshoes up on the lawn and the women washed dishes in the kitchen, the children toasted marshmallows over a small fire on the beach.

While any sort of confection was a treat in those quiet years between the War and the Great Depression, a bag of marshmallows was a treasure almost beyond imagining. But Uncle Joe knew a man who worked in a candy factory in Massachusetts, and that man had given Uncle Joe a bag of marshmallows one morning on the train, and Uncle Joe had brought that bag to upstate New York in July

of 1932. There were about fifty marshmallows in the bag by cousin
Gene's count, and there were seven cousins. Gene, the oldest at 13,
sketched complicated equations in the damp sand, calculating with
authority that each cousin should receive eight and three-quarters
marshmallows. Six sets of sand-dusted hands reached out to receive
their bounty of puffed white sugar: Kathryn with her blond hair in
pigtails; Howard and Ivan, each wearing a single shoe; George, just
five, who had recently survived chicken pox and was still spotted
with crusty scabs; and Evelyn, the second oldest, who secretly
questioned her brother's mathematical aptitude but took her eight-
and-three-quarters without complaint. Gene's calculations being
slightly off, only four rather smallish marshmallows remained in the
bag after he had taken his own. He turned to Edward, who had been
gazing into the fire, and said: "Want the rest?"

And Edward said: "Yes."

He spoke again that night, laying in the grass in the backyard,
under a bright canopy of stars and a small fingernail moon. The
younger children had been sent in to bed, but Edward, Evelyn, and
Gene had been granted permission to camp out. They had at first
sprawled themselves across the yard, each taking up as much space
as possible, arranging their rough grain sack beddings just so, placing

shoes and socks at even intervals to mark boundaries. But after the last light in the house had been extinguished, and the sounds of night—water lapping against the dock, crickets calling from the long grass near the shed, something small but quick scampering through the garden—closed in around them, they drew close together, and finally ended up in a tight row, looking up at the stars.

"Can I see your toe?" Evelyn whispered. It was not lost on her that Edward wore his clunky brown shoes even when they were playing on the beach.

"Sure," Edward said, and that was word number two.

The night sky offered little in the way of light, but Gene and Evelyn could still make out the missing piece of Edward's left foot. They marveled as he wiggled the remaining digits, and asked many questions: Did the little stump itch? Was it hard to run? Could he still swim?

Edward answered their questions easily enough. If he experienced any trouble with his voice after nearly five months of disuse, it was not apparent to his cousins. When Evelyn and Gene had exhausted their questions, they lay silently for some time. A small orange cat by the name of Lou wandered over and made a place for herself behind Evelyn's knees.

Just as Edward was about to close his eyes, Gene said: "Tell us what happened, won't you?"

If his mother and father, settling down for the night, heard the sound of their son's voice and sat up in bed, clasping hands in joy and surprise, they gave no sign.

The next morning at breakfast—fresh blueberry muffins and strong coffee—Edward's mother may have betrayed her surprise with a small twitch of her hand, which upset the creamer, but she said nothing. Edward's father, once a blustery man prone to exaggeration and exclamation, raised an eyebrow.

\*\*\*

On the morning of February 6, 1932, Edward and Thomas Sorensen woke to find six inches of freshly fallen snow standing between themselves and a day of ice-skating on the lake. The new snow meant shoveling the driveway, the path to the shed, both porches, the dock, and the driveway and porches of Old Man Winter next door. Then, after the shoveling was complete, there was brushing off to be done: the car, Old Man Winter's car (which he never drove and which, Thomas discovered sometime during January break, had sunk half a foot into the ground during the long December rains and was now frozen in place), the dog house roof, the chicken coop roof, Old Man Winter's chicken coop roof, and anything else from which their mother, gazing out the kitchen window as she peeled potatoes for supper, saw fit to remove the snow.

After snow chores there were usual Saturday chores: collecting the day's eggs, cleaning out the chicken coop, walking the dog—a chore that fell to Edward and which he particularly loathed, given that the dog had free reign of the property all day and could therefore, technically, walk himself—hauling the garbage to the compost pile, and walking the quarter-mile to Millard's and back for a week's worth of butter and milk.

There was a brief respite for lunch: hunks of cold beef on crusty bread, and warm oatmeal cookies fresh from the oven. Then it was time for homework; Thomas had twice as much as Edward, which Thomas found to be quite unfair, and so he caused a fight that ended with a half hour of standing in the corner for both.

And so it was after four o'clock before the brothers finally put on their heavy coats and wool mittens and allowed their mother to place matching red wool hats upon their heads. Their father had sharpened their skates that morning; Edward's drew blood on the pad of his thumb when he tested it "to be sure it was ready." A bandage later and the boys were on the ice, 75 feet from the shore, hockey sticks in hand.

Hockey had become an obsession the winter before, when a family of four boys, the Morehouses, arrived on the lake one snowy morning and invited Thomas and Edward out to play. For three months the boys chased each other back and forth between two homemade goals, brandishing broomsticks with gusto, if not grace. Their grandfather had given them the hockey sticks for Christmas. Finally.

A stiff wind had picked up, freezing the top layer of snow to an icy crust. The Morehouse boys were not around, but after twenty minutes or so Steven Tomion and Sam Martin skated over. The noise of the game attracted several on-lookers, among them Rachael Tomion, Steven's older sister and the object of Thomas's current crush, and Olivia with the unpronounceable last name, who had moved away to California and then come back again the previous spring. Butch Hollowell, the most talented hockey player on the eastern branch of the lake, arrived at the game with a handful of boys from Hammondsport. They'd been ice fishing near the Bluff for most of the day, and along with their hockey sticks and homemade shin guards, they brought with them several good-sized trout gasping their last breaths in a large brown basket.

Edward remembers only flashes of the game: Sam Martin getting an elbow in the eye and doing an admirable job of not crying; Rachael cheering when Thomas scored; the look of horror on Thomas's face when the ice cracked beneath Edward's feet and he went under.

He smacked his head on the way down, a good crack on the right temple, but he didn't pass out. He was in the water and under the ice, and he could see boots above him, and a bright red blur that was Thomas's hat, or maybe Butch's scarf. More ice cracked then, and the boots were gone. Muffled, distant, came the sound of someone screaming. Then a hand grabbed the top of Edward's head and pulled. Only his hat was rescued.

The gloveless hand came down again. Edward saw the ghostly outline of his brother's face—he'd lost his glasses in the fall; everything was blurry, but that was also the water, of course—and could see his brother's lips forming words: "Help," "God," and, over and over: "No."

Edward felt a tug on the top of his head. He kicked with his skates, willing himself to the surface. But instead of Edward reaching the surface, Thomas was down in the lake with him. They looked at each other through the murky water. Thomas gave Edward a thumbs' up, reached down into the darkness beneath him, wrapped his arms around Edward's knees, and gave him a violent shove.

Edward's body belched onto the ice. He could feel his left skate dangling into the water, but found that he couldn't move his leg.

"Oh no oh no oh no," Rachael said from somewhere very close by.

"Get back!"

It was Edward's father, his deep voice booming, silencing Rachael's litany and sending a flock of crows into the darkening sky. Edward saw his father's face come into focus just above his. He smelled pipe tobacco and something sweet but old, like cinnamon, and felt his father's rough mustache press against his lips. Hot air poured down his throat.

"Breathe, son," his father ordered.

"I am," Edward tried to say, and passed out.

Thomas never surfaced; his body was found lodged against the entrance to the Outlet during the spring thaw, and he was buried next to Grandfather Sorensen in mid-April.

\*\*\*

In the dark of the summer night, as Edward's voice at last grew raspy and faded to silence, Evelyn reached out and placed the last marshmallow in the palm of Edward's hand.

# The Stone Wife

Danny watched the rain spill over the edge of the dugout and onto the dirt floor. Saturdays were usually his favorite, but this was the worst. Totally beyond boring. He stomped on a puddle and got mud all over his new sneakers and on his legs and knees. That would get Julie mad for sure.

Dad had dropped him off at quarter of just like every Saturday. It was only cloudy then, gray and sticky but not raining yet. Danny was usually the first one at practice anyway, because Dad had to be at work by nine. The other guys usually started showing up about ten minutes later. But now Danny's watch said 9:12 and still nobody else was there. They weren't stupid enough to come to practice when it was pouring.

He could walk home. It was only three blocks up and two over. Or, he could dig up a quarter and use the old pay phone next to the concession stand and see if Julie was back from dropping stupid Evvie at the stupid Girl Scouts bake sale down at the P&C. Of course then Julie would yell at him for ruining her schedule. She loved schedules. She would probably kiss a schedule if she could.

He looked around half-heartedly for a quarter, or a bunch of nickels, or something, but the dugout was empty except for him and the mud puddles and a wadded up roster from last week's game. The game where Danny walked six guys from Morgan's Grocery but also won the game with a triple in the bottom of the ninth. That had been an awesome game. Which of course Dad missed because Julie made him go visit her sister in the hospital.

Danny put his glove on his head and leaned back against the wall. Sometimes, when you couldn't decide what to do, the best thing was to just sit and wait. Sooner or later, you'd figure out what you were supposed to do.

The rain was really starting to come down. Danny could barely see the ads for The Wagner and Long's Cards & Books along the center-field fence.

"Yo."

Danny swallowed a shout. He pulled his glove off his head and punched it twice with his fist. "Hello?"

A tall kid with black hair swooped around the corner and slid onto the bench next to Danny.

"You the only one here?"

Danny nodded. The kid didn't have a glove or hat or cleats or anything. Just blue jeans with holes in the knees and a faded red t-shirt with an Indian chief on it.

"Pretty crappy day for baseball."

"Yeah." Danny stuck out his hand, the one without the glove. "I'm Danny."

"Kevin," he said, and pumped Danny's hand up and down once. "Nice glove."

"Thanks."

Danny showed Kevin the autographs: Jeter, Giambi, A-Rod. It was his most prized possession, better than the football autographed by Brett Favre or the hundred dollar bill Grandpa had given him on his tenth birthday. Julie had made him put that in the bank, anyway.

"Must be worth something, with those. They old?" Kevin touched the autographs, black swooshes on the brown leather. His fingers were short and thick, like sausages.

"My dad got them a bunch of years ago."

"I could sell it online for you."

Danny took the glove back and tucked it up under his leg. "No, thanks. My dad would kill me."

Kevin said, "Okay."

They sat in a not-too-uncomfortable silence for a few minutes, while the rain beat down louder on the tin roof. Danny thought about asking Kevin if he had a quarter he could borrow, but just then Kevin said, "You wanna go over there?" He stuck out his sausage pointer finger.

"The cemetery?"

Kevin laughed, a sound like coughing in the back of his throat. "Yeah." He looked over at Danny and smiled. He was missing two teeth on the bottom. "If you dare." He waved his hands and made what was probably supposed to be a scary face and said, "Oooooooo."

Danny laughed. "I'm not scared. It's wet, though. Probably muddy."

"I'll show you some cool stuff, though. Ever see the Stone Wife?"

Kevin was already up and splashing through the puddles behind home plate. Danny took his cap out of his back pocket and crammed it onto his head.

There wasn't any traffic to worry about as they dashed across East Elm. Danny headed toward the main gate, but Kevin grabbed his arm and yanked him to the left. "Don't go by the house, we'll get caught."

"We're not doing anything wrong."

"Yeah, but we don't need McMinn knowing we're in here."

"Who's McMinn?"

Kevin rolled his eyes. "The caretaker."

They slipped and slid in the wet grass along the wrought-iron fence. Just before they reached the side gate, out of view from the caretaker's house, Danny's sneaker slipped in the mud and he went down hard on his right knee. There wasn't too much blood.

Kevin waited for him under a big maple with low branches, just inside the gate. His black hair was plastered to his forehead and neck; he shook his head like a dog.

Danny bent over, his hands planted just above his bloody knee. He took a minute to catch his breath and then said, "Okay, who's the Stone Wife?"

"It's not a who, it's a what. Or both, I guess." Kevin took a wrinkled package out of his back pocket. He dug out a clump of pink gum and stuck it in his cheek. "Want some?" he asked.

Danny dug a wad of gum out and stuck it in his cheek, too. Julie hardly ever let them chew gum, especially not the sugary, sticky kind like Big League. He stuck his tongue into the middle of it and blew a giant bubble.

"Stone Wife is a grave," Kevin said. He hunched down, his back against the trunk of the old tree. "Up the main hill, about a quarter mile from the road. It's black, about so big—"

Kevin stretched out his arms as far as they would go.

"And it's got a face on it."

Danny crouched down, too. He whispered, "A face?"

"Face of the woman who's buried there. Her name is Matilda, and she haunts the grave trying to get back at her husband."

Danny looked down at the grass between his feet so Kevin wouldn't see how all the color had drained out of his cheeks. He picked dirt out of the cut on his knee.

Kevin said, "He cheated on her and gambled and drank and did all this stuff a husband shouldn't do. So she was dying one day, she was only like twenty-five or something, and she raised up her finger and pointed at Frank (that was the husband's name) and said, 'You'll never get rid of me, I'll have my eye on you in this life and beyond!' Or something like that. And then she died."

Kevin stood up so suddenly that Danny gasped, rocked back on his heels, and fell butt first on the soggy ground. Kevin laughed his weird, throaty laugh and helped Danny up.

They started up the long sloping hill at an angle. The rain was coming down worse than before, but they were mostly under trees, so just a few fat drops landed on their shoulders. As they walked, Kevin told the rest of the story.

"Frank, the husband, bought a big old black stone for her grave stone, with room enough so that when he died, they could put his name on it, too. And they buried her up on the hill, high enough and away from the trees so that she could see clear over to the lake, since that was her favorite place."

Kevin stopped and looked back at Danny, whose sneakers were slipping on the slick grass. "I'm coming," Danny said. He was panting a little now. Kevin's legs were a lot longer than his.

"So they bury her, and three days later, Frank comes by to leave some flowers by the grave. And when he gets there, he sees The Face."

Danny shivered, and rubbed at the goose bumps that covered his arms. "The Face?" His voice went up an octave.

Kevin stopped, waited for Danny to catch up, and put a hand on Danny's shoulder. He leaned close, so that Danny could smell Kevin's baloney-and-Dr.-Pepper breakfast. Kevin closed his eyes and said the next part in almost a whisper, and also like he was reciting something they'd made him learn in school:

"A white mark had appeared on the grave, in the shape of Matilda's face. Her eyes, her nose, her long hair curled over her shoulder, everything. It hadn't been there the day they buried her, but it was there now. Frank got down on his knee and touched the part of the face that was Matilda's cheek. And that's when it happened."

Danny tried to take a step back, but Kevin tightened the grip on his shoulder and leaned in closer.

"She slapped him."

"What? How?"

Kevin started walking again, moving quickly around a broken headstone and a half-buried pot of mums. "Well, I don't know exactly how it works, but basically they say that whatever part of the face you touch, you get beat on that same place on your own face."

"So it's a ghost. A poltergeist or something."

"Do you believe in ghosts?"

"I don't know. I mean, I've never seen one."

"Your folks grow up around here? I bet your dad and his friends came here and tried it."

"Tried what?"

"Touching the stone. Tons of people come in here to try, but hardly anyone ever gets up the guts to really do it. My dad did, once."

Kevin was almost running now, and Danny couldn't keep up. He stopped next to a tall grave that looked like the Washington Monument. He cupped his hands around his mouth and called, "What happened?"

Kevin turned and jogged back. He wasn't even out of breath.

"He touched her neck, and then something touched his neck. He said it was like a hand made of ice. It left big purple bruises, about the size of a lady's hand."

They looked at each other.

"You don't believe me."

"Do you have a picture or anything?"

"Naw. He was only our age, maybe a little older. They didn't even have cameras then."

Danny laughed, but Kevin scowled. "Yes they did. Your dad can't be much older than mine, and he has tons of pictures from when he was a kid."

Kevin turned his back. "They didn't have a camera. But I believe him. He gets this look in his eyes when he talks about that night—"

"They went in at night?"

Kevin wheeled around again, smiling this time. The gap in his bottom teeth looked bigger somehow. "Yeah, him and his two best friends snuck in a couple of nights before Halloween. They put on all black and snuck in from the entrance over on Rosewood, you know the one I mean?" Danny didn't, but he nodded anyway. "My dad touched the neck and felt the icy hand on his throat. Then his friend Gene touched the eye, and wham! Black eye. The other kid was this guy named Mac. He was gonna touch the nose, but then McMinn showed up. He was the caretaker even back then. He came running at them with a flashlight and a shovel, and chased them out the front gate."

Kevin stopped and grinned down at Danny.

"Wow."

"Heh, yeah." Kevin stuck his hands into the pockets of his ripped up jeans and said, "You ready? It's just over there, behind that crypt thingie."

Danny did not want to go. He wanted to go back to the dugout and see if any of the guys had shown up, maybe throw a ball around. Or he could just sit in the dugout and work his glove and wait for his dad to show up. What time was it, anyway? It might be close to eleven already, and if he wasn't there when Dad showed up, everyone would get panicky and Julie would call the cops and Evvie would cry and it would be a big mess and it would be all his fault.

"You're chicken, aren't you?"

Danny's back stiffened. "Am not."

"Then let's go."

They crossed the dirt path and edged around the crypt. The hair on the back of Danny's neck stood up when the back of the stone came into view. It wasn't as big as Kevin said it was, but it was big enough. Jet black, too, slick and shiny from the rain.

Kevin walked around to the front of the grave. He spread his feet apart and folded his arms across his chest. Danny looked past him, down the hill and across the ball field to the lake. It was flat and silver and silent. No jet skiers or speed boats on a day like this.

Danny took a deep breath and took five slow steps closer to Kevin. He closed his eyes, and when he did, Kevin grabbed his shoulders and spun him around so he was facing the grave.

"Look, come on!"

Danny peeked.

It was a face. A side view of a woman with a pointy chin and long curly hair. She was looking back over her shoulder, the way girls posed for school pictures. There was a dark blotch that was her eye, and a little curve that was her ear.

"Are you sure it wasn't made this way?"

"Positive."

"It looks like it was."

Kevin held up three fingers. "Scouts' honor."

Danny laughed and pretended to throw a punch. "Yeah, you're a Boy Scout, I bet."

Kevin snorted. "But you are, right?"

Danny blushed. "My dad's the leader." He bent over to get a better look at the face. "Well, okay. It totally looks like a lady's face."

"Touch it."

"No way."

"Come on."

"You touch it."

Danny wasn't sure who started it, but there was a lot of pushing and shoving and some pretty bad swear words, and then Kevin rushed at him and socked him right in the guts with the top of his head. Danny went down in a heap, and before he realized what was happening, his hand flew back and to the left, and he smacked the Stone Wife right in the mouth.

"Ow!" Danny gasped. He put his hand on his face. Blood! He looked up at Kevin, who was backing away. "Did you punch me in the face?"

"I didn't hit you. It's her!" Kevin pointed at the stone.

Danny backpedaled away from the grave, his butt and sneakers sliding in the mud. "Help me up!" He swiped at the blood trickling from his split lip.

Kevin said, "By the way, thanks," and plucked Danny's glove from the grass where it had landed during the fight.

"Wait. Help me up, give me that back!"

Kevin backed away, laughing his low, croaky laugh. "Stupid kid."

Danny grabbed a headstone and pulled himself to his feet. Blood trickled from his lip onto his jersey. Julie was going to be steaming mad about that. Blood was harder to get out even than grass stains, she said. He took a step toward Kevin. His sneaker slipped on the wet grass and he started to go down.

He saw it in slow-motion: He was going to hit his head on that stumpy grave with the little lamb on the top, and then he was going to pass out and Kevin was going to run off with his glove. And when someone finally found him, probably hours from now, he was going to get spanked and grounded. No doubt about it.

A pair of hands grabbed him under the armpits and yanked him back to his feet.

"Run," a scratchy voice said. Danny didn't have to be told twice.

But the voice didn't mean him, because when he went to move, a hand came down on the back of his neck and squeezed. "Go now, Kevin."

"Yes, sir," Kevin said, his voice almost a whisper. All the color had drained from his face. He held up the glove, dark brown now from the rain. "Can I keep it?"

"Of course," the scratchy voice said. "You've earned it. Now go."

"That stupid story works every time," Kevin said. He shook his head, water flying from his black hair. "A ghost in a grave that hits you back. I can't believe people actually believe it!"

The hand on Danny's neck squeezed harder. "I said go."

Kevin's laugh stopped mid-croak. He turned around in a weird robotic way and ran away down the hill to the main gate.

There was hot breath in Danny's ear. The hand on the back of his neck relaxed, but didn't go away. From the corner of his eye, Danny saw the bright yellow of a rain coat, and something silver. A shovel?

"Mister, that kid took my glove."

The silver thing moved. It was definitely a shovel. It was

McMinn, it had to be. Of course a cemetery caretaker would have a shovel. Danny tried to turn around, but the hand on the back of his neck squeezed again.

"It's just, that's a real special glove. To me, I mean. It's autographed from when Dad went to Yankee Stadium one time. I need to get it back."

The hot breath sighed in his ear. "You don't need to worry about that."

Danny's heart thudded in his chest. He was more scared than he'd ever been, more than when Mom left, more than when he accidentally pushed Evvie down the stairs at the cottage and she broke her arm. He tried to take a deep breath, but his lungs were full of cement.

He could make a run for it, he was wet and slippery and could just wriggle out of McMinn's hand—

"Don't make me hurt you," McMinn said. "Now walk."

The shovel pressed into Danny's back. He walked. They went deeper into the cemetery, where the trees were thicker and no one would be able to see them from the road. When they crested the hill, McMinn yanked Danny to a stop.

"In there," he said, and pointed at a rusty green shed.

"Mister, please. Just let me go. I won't tell anybody, I promise."

"Get inside and shut your mouth."

Danny turned. He wasn't going to go in that shed. If he did, he'd die. McMinn raised the shovel. He swung hard, and his boots slipped in the slick grass. He went down, his yellow raincoat flying out behind him. Danny bolted.

Down the hill, skidding around the Stone Wife, past the Washington Monument. The rain fell harder. Danny blinked furiously to keep the water out of his eyes. He didn't turn when he heard McMinn behind him, grunting and coughing, his shovel clanging against the graves.

Run, run. Dad wouldn't care about the glove. He would only care that Danny was safe and unhurt. They would file a police report. Maybe they'd never see the glove again. Jeter, Giambi, A-Rod. Jeter, Giambi, A-Rod. Run, run.

Danny veered to the right, his feet more sure on the gravel of the driveway. He was sprinting now, his breath hot and tight in his chest. Not far to the gate—first to third, that was all—then across Elm and into the park. Was that Julie's car down there, parked just outside the concession stand?

He screamed her name. Did she look? Did she turn her head?

No, it was too far and it was raining too hard. He screamed again, louder. This time she definitely looked. He was at the gate, hands slipping on the wrought-iron bars. Locked!

"Danny?" Julie's voice carried to him through the rain. He rattled the bars, his teeth snapping together. "Danny?" She was mad.

He screamed her name again, the loudest scream of his life. His throat felt like fire. But Julie didn't look around again. She was talking to someone, a tall kid with black hair and a red t-shirt. And a glove. She would see the glove! She hated baseball, but she knew the glove, they all knew that glove. Even Julie knew Jeter, Giambi, A-Rod.

"Bad boy," McMinn said.

Danny saw the glint of sliver as the shovel came down.

# Through the Storm

I nearly lost my eye the day the Good Lord Jesus took John away, finally. Gram said it was him that sent the lightning that split the tree, which came right in the window and nearly killed us both as we were saying goodnight to John. Like uninvited company just when you are sitting down to supper.

Glass went in my hair and down my nightshirt and one piece stuck in the skin next to my right eye, so that I didn't dare blink and was afraid to even move, until Gram shouted to stay with John and she ran down to check the generator.

It was pitch-dark except the lightning, which lit up John's face like a mask on Halloween, his black eyes staring up at nothing and his mouth pulled away from the breathing tube like he would scream if he had a voice. I could only see him out of one eye, what with the blood sliding down my face, but I didn't dare wipe it away, because of the glass.

I squeezed John's hand and prayed to the Good Lord Jesus to see us through the storm, both the one outside and the one in our lives every day, which was John never getting better and never getting worse, just breathing steady thanks to the machine and, Gram said, our love.

The tree that we climbed every summer up until his accident was right there in the room with the two of us, the branch with the rope grown into the bark smashed on top of the machine that made John breathe. Thunder boomed the loudest yet, and John twitched a little, or maybe that was me.

"Dead!" Gram shouted over the noise. She leaned against the chair, panting and holding her left arm funny to her chest. "I can't get it started."

We looked at each other across the bed. No power and no gen-

erator meant no machine, and no machine meant no breath
for John.

I said, "What do we do?" and Gram said, "Pray," but not
for what.

There was nothing to do and no one to call, so we lit a lantern
Gram kept for emergencies and she took the breathing tube out of
John's mouth and there he was, looking finally like my brother again,
except softer at the edges, like he'd spent too long in the bathtub.
His mouth worked like a fish, and then he settled.

We perched each on one side of the bed, and held his hands
in ours, and whispered prayers. After a while, the rain started,
splattering in the dust under the window that was now just a hole in
the house with a tree sticking through it. John started to shift around
and moan a little then, the first noise he'd made in a year.

"Go on now," Gram said, and smoothed his hair back from
his face. "Don't be afraid, John." There was a hitch in her voice
when she said his name, I heard it over the thunder. How was John
supposed to be brave when Gram was scared? I tried to swallow, but
my tongue filled up my mouth.

John didn't so much as look at Gram, but his eyes flickered over
and he looked at me.

"What?" I asked. "Tell me. I won't forget." I leaned close, so close the glass near my eye touched his cheek, but all he did was breathe once on my face, hot and thick like he'd been rolled up in a rug and stuffed in the back of a closet half his life. And then John stopped.

After that, Gram brought the lantern close and plucked the glass out of my eye without telling me what she was up to. The blood gushed onto John's shirt, but Gram said leave it 'til morning, leave it all 'til morning.

We laid in her bed, Gram with her arm wrapped up and pressed close to her chest, me with a bandage taped over my eye, and listened to the rain come down on the roof and the yard and the busted car in the driveway, on the barn with the lonesome dog that wouldn't let anybody pet her anymore, on the mailbox with the flag rusted up forever like we were putting out mail every day, sending letters to the whole world.

In the next room, just the other side of the plaster wall, my brother John was dead at last, the Good Lord Jesus finally heard my prayer and took him away. I snuggled close to Gram, her body hot like a coal from the stove, and put my hand on that soft secret place under her chin.

The rain came hard and steady, and even though I knew the machine was busted, I could still hear it breathing in the next room, never stopping, the hum running under all the days of our lives, keeping John alive. But no, John was dead. Amen.

Gram started to sing, deep in her throat, summertime, and the livin' is easy. The low rumble of notes traveled up my wrist to my elbow and straight into my heart, where I stoppered it up quick and hid it away for other stormy nights ahead.

In the morning, Gram's side of the bed was empty and cool. I laid quiet with my eyes closed, listening to the tinkle of glass as she swept up on the other side of the wall. Warm sun filled the room and lit up the bloody bandage over my eye, turning the whole world red as my beating heart.

# A Better End

When you have a story that is about two people, for the story to be anything worth reading, in the end the two people either have to end up in love or dead. It's best if they end up married, or if just one of them lives—that makes for an even better story that people will remember and tell their friends. So, having said that, you know to expect love or death by the end of this. But I won't give away which.

John made the chicken wings extra hot on Friday nights, because that's when the crowd came over after the races over at Black Rock, covered in track dust and sweat, and pressed their bellies against the bar and John would line up rows of ice cold brews, usually Coors Light but sometimes Michelob or Pabst Blue Ribbon. Since I'm off school for the summer, I used to work breakfast on Friday, but at the end of June Cathy quit to have a baby so John put me on the dinner shift, which was good for extra tips especially if a local had won at the races, which he had this Friday.

I knew or recognized by face about half the guys that night. There was Tom and Tim Walker, the twins from Dresden who owned all the gas stations around town, and Pastor Ken who wasn't a pastor of anything that anybody knew of. Next to him, stuffing chicken wings in his fat mouth like they were going out of style yesterday was Larry Hansen. He went off and got a degree at a school out in Boston and came home and said everyone was supposed to call him Dr. Laurence Hansen now but nobody did. He hadn't done anything with it, just hung that piece of paper on the wall at his mom and dad's and spent his days reading books and his nights drinking at the bar and hitting on everyone, especially me.

Next to Larry was a tall drink of water I had never seen before but I decided right off I would like to see looking at me across the breakfast table at home for the rest of my life.

He was tall, as I have said, and skinny in a kind of nice way that made me think I could fatten him up with a few Sunday turkey dinners and some meatloaf sandwiches. He had long hair, brown with some gray in it, that he had tucked behind his ears so I could see just the side of his face from where I was delivering fish frys to the Mortensens and their snotty grandkids.

I couldn't get a good look at his face until I went behind the bar, but I needed a reason to go behind the bar because I didn't want him to think I was going back there just to look at him, even though I was. Also, I didn't want to have to talk to Larry. He asks me out once a week, and I always turn him down of course. He has a belly like he's ten months pregnant, and he smells like beef jerky and Irish Spring. Not to mention he has tiny hands, pink and soft like a little girl would have. From school and practice and work, my hands are rough and dry, but I at least lotion them up before I go to bed. Which goes to prove how much work Larry does, and I'm ten years younger.

So I had to find a way to get a good look at the new guy while at the same time avoiding Larry. Which the solution for fell into my lap when Larry let out a giant disgusting belch and announced to everyone in earshot and beyond that he was going to take a leak.

I went quick behind the bar and walked right up to the guy and said, "Coffee?" even though I didn't have any coffee to give him.

Also, he wasn't drinking coffee. None of them were. They were drinking beers, and a lot of them. He looked at me with the most heart-melting blue-green eyes, crinkled at the corners like crepe paper wadded up in a corner after a keg party. He smiled, and my heart did a little skip when I saw that he had all his teeth.

"I'll have another Coors, if you're serving," he said. He took a rubber band out of his pocket and whipped his hair into a ponytail just as good as I could. He was even handsomer that way, with the hair out of his face. He looked serious and important, except for his smiling eyes.

His voice was deep, too, and I thought if his voice was a thing I would wrap myself up in it like a fuzzy blanket on a frosty night. Plus, he said a complete sentence that sounded right grammar-wise, which is more than I can say for most of the yokels up in this place. Except Larry, who has a degree.

"I'll get John," I said in a kind of mumble. I have been told by more than one man that I have a really sexy voice, but something about the way the new guy was smiling at me made my throat feel like it was lined with sand paper. The kind you use to get old green paint off the side of a boat.

"I can see the bottles right there," he said, and leaned over the bar and brushed his arm against mine to point at the fridge full of cold Coors Light bottles. The hair on my arm stood up. The hair everywhere on my everything stood up.

"I can't serve you," I said, after I coughed a little to make my voice sound like its usually sexy self. "I'm seventeen."

Usually I wait until the second date to lay that one on them. I look a lot older than I am—like at least twenty-two. One guy, an accountant who was in town to do an audit at the hospital last fall, said he thought I looked like his sister, who was twenty-five. I don't know about that, but I'm glad at least that I look old enough so I don't get carded when I buy beer over in Geneva where they don't know me.

"Seventeen," the guy repeated, and sat back down on the stool. He picked up a piece of celery and chewed on it a little. He hadn't touched the bleu cheese.

"I'm out of school," I said like an idiot, which I am not. But sometimes there are certain men that make me slow and thick in the brain. That hadn't happened in awhile—not since Chaz, and we all know how that ended up. I mean, those of us who need to know,

know. Everyone else can mind their business.

"I'm out of school, too," he said.

Larry was on his way back from the restroom. As usual, I could hear him before I could see him. I knew this was my only chance, so I stood up on my tiptoes, leaned over the bar, and whispered in the new guy's ear: "I get off at one o'clock."

If I'd said that to Larry, he would have said, "I get off all day," or something else stupid that you wouldn't expect someone with a degree to say. That was Larry, though. He might be a doctor, but he was still a jerk. The new guy smiled, showing me all his teeth again, and nodded. It was a little nod, one you wouldn't notice unless you were looking real close, but I was, so I saw it.

I won't bore you with the rest of the night. It was just chicken wing sauce on my apron and spilled beer on the floor and a burn on my arm from the deep fryer where John was cooking up batch after batch of french fries. Larry hit on me three times before John shoved him out the door after last call. I watched him through the window, stumbling to the parking lot. One day, he'd wrap his fancy Camry with the leather seats around a tree, and I for one would not be in line at the funeral home to say goodbye to his closed coffin.

So at about five after one I followed John and Wendy and Kiki and Vic out the back door and past the dumpsters. Kiki and Wendy got into Kiki's car and drove away; they were never friendly with me, because I am so much prettier and popular than them and always have been. Vic, who is like a grandpa to me, asked me if I needed a ride. But I saw the new guy leaning up against the fence just past where the street lights stopped, and I told Vic no, I was going to walk since it was such a mild and nice night out.

I waited until I couldn't hear his and John's cars any more, and then I walked over to the guy as fast as I could without it looking like I was running, which I wanted to.

"Hey," he said. He had a brown cigarette in his hand. I don't mind smoking.

"Hi there," I said, just as casual as can be. The sandpaper sound was out of my throat, finally.

"Well," he said, and kicked the curb with the toe of his boot. It was a cowboy boot, tan with black stitching on it. "What do we do now?"

I put out my hand, which I had thankfully just painted the nails on last week and they weren't too chewed up. "I'm Stacey," I said. We shook, and then he said: "I'm David."

I moved a little closer to him, not because it was cold, but to let him know I wanted to be closer to him. He dropped the cigarette and put his arm around my waist. I have always been proud of my waist, which is hardly bigger around than a basketball. Except when I got knocked up, but thanks to Chaz that got taken care of fast, the only thing I am glad of him for.

"Want to drive out to the lake?" he said, and his voice was loud in the dark parking lot. He pointed at his car, which was a beat-up Ford pickup with the front fender missing. I don't care much about cars, as long as they get you to where you need to go, which is why I wasn't impressed by Larry's heated seats or moon roof the one time I let him take me to the movies. The one and only time, since he tried to feel me up during the previews.

I sat next to David on the drive out to the lake, my leg pressed right up against his. He put some sexy music on the radio, a black guy singing in a high voice about undressing his woman and making sweet love to her. I wriggled a little closer to David.

He pulled into a parking area that I'd been to more than once before, under a broken light so we were in the dark. There were some stars out, and lights in the cottages on the water.

"You're a pretty thing," David said, and put his arm around my shoulders. He leaned in to kiss me and I could smell something on him that reminded me of pennies. His lips were soft but the stubble on his chin and cheeks was going to give me a burn. Guys never think about those things.

We kissed for awhile, and then I knew he was ready for more and his hands were going everywhere very fast. I pushed him away and put my back against the passenger door and asked him if he had anything to drink. It's always a good idea to let a man simmer for awhile.

He got some beers out from a cooler behind the seat, and we sat in the dark and drank them. The sound of his breathing was heavy and loud, but not enough to cover up my heart, which was racing like Miss G had just made me run laps for being late to practice. I usually wasn't nervous about doing it with a guy. I drank all of the beer, even though it was warm.

"Okay," David said. He opened his door and got out. I followed him around to the bed of the truck, which had no tailgate. I hopped up and sat, swinging my feet. "Lay down," he said.

I looked behind me but there was nothing but some old paint cans and a tarp and a tool box. I laughed, and my laugh is deep and sexy. "I don't think so," I said, and tossed my hair. My hair is long and brown, and I deep condition it two times a week, Tuesdays and

Saturdays, which is tomorrow.

"Lay down," David said again. He got between my legs and pushed me back. My head bonked against the metal bed. "Be quiet."

"I'm not quiet," I said, leaning up on my elbows. That made my cleavage look even bigger. It got big when I got pregnant, and stayed big even after, for which everyone was pretty much grateful, except maybe Kiki and Wendy. "I'm noisy," I said, and giggled to show how fun I was.

David kissed me again, rougher this time. I do like it rough, I admit. A man who takes charge and tells a woman what to do is my kind of man. "If you aren't quiet," he said, "someone will hear you."

He climbed up on top of me and kissed me for awhile. I tried to unbutton his jeans but he pushed my hands away. I looked up at the stars while he kissed my neck. Sometimes, there are men you just can't figure out.

"What do you do?" I asked.

"I'm a carpenter," he said.

"Like Jesus."

"Just like Jesus. Shut up."

"You don't know how to treat a woman," I said, and tried to

sit up, but he kept me pinned down with his arm across my chest. "I bet you haven't had many girlfriends if that's the way you treat a woman."

I was mad now, and when I get mad I get mouthy, which David was about to find out. I opened my mouth to give him more business, and that's when he shoved a rag in my mouth. The turpentine made me gag, but I couldn't spit it out. He leaned down close so that we were eye to eye. Through the reek of the rag I could smell pennies again.

As his hands closed around my throat, David said in a whisper: "My wife thinks I treat her just fine."

And so you see, I haven't lied. When you have a story that is about two people, for the story to be anything worth reading, in the end the two people either have to end up in love or dead. David is in love, and now I'm dead.

# Another Night at the All-you-can-Eat Buffet

Friday nights suck. I should be out with the girls, but no, I was the last busser hired for the summer so I get stuck with the crap shifts. But I guess it's not so bad because Friday nights have the best tippers. My first paycheck I used to buy the sweetest pair of four-and-a-half-inch red patent leather Steve Madden heels. Kyle really loves them, especially when they're the only thing I'm wearing.

Okay, shoes or no shoes, I should be working at Unique Boutique with Jess and Tracy. It's the best summer job, great hours, you just wait on rich ladies all day and it's right next to the coffee shop and you can totally get free cappuccino if you flirt with the guy behind the counter. But anyway, best of all, they close at six on Fridays, whereas the buffet's open till eleven. Still, it was totally worth it to miss getting that job because I was in Puerto Rico with Kyle and his step-mom when they were hiring for summer sales girls. PR was so awesome. God, the shopping! And the food... Lobster tails thick as my wrist, huge juicy slabs of filet mignon, and mountains of fresh guacamole. God, I love guacamole. Not that I ate a lot of it. But Kyle thought it was delicious.

So Fridays suck, but at least this is my last one. Five more hours and I'm done with Stan and Jan's Route 14A All-You-Can-Eat Buffet. No more musty dish towels, no more mustard crusted under my fingernails, no more screaming kids making hand prints in the soft serve ice cream they smear all over the tables that I have to clean up. And especially no more Gerry.

Gerry is fat. Not just fat—huge. Nearly as big as Mom got before she died, and she was over 350. That's as high as the scale went, anyway.

Gerry comes in every Friday night between five thirty and six. He always sits in the same booth, the one they fixed up with a regular chair because there's no way he could squeeze his gut into a normal booth. Mom was the same. We didn't go to the movies or out to eat for ages after she started getting really big. She got to the point where she wouldn't even go to Sammy's Little League games, which just had bleachers so I'm not sure what the deal was with that.

"Hello, Heather," Gerry says to me. I'm scraping a meatloaf and mashed potato mess off table eight. "How goes it?"

"It's all right," I say. I don't want to make eye contact with Gerry. I hate how puffy his cheeks are, like the fat in them is taking over his face, eating up his eyes. Mom was fat all over, round as a balloon, but with Gerry you really notice it in his head. Like a cantaloupe that's about to burst.

"I'll have a chocolate milkshake today, I think." He says the same thing every Friday, like he might one day ask for vanilla or strawberry even though I know he won't, and he knows it, too. Another thing is, he always tries to talk to me. He's always asking things like how lacrosse is going and where I'm gonna go to college and how my brother is. He and Mom were in the same class at York High, so that makes him think he knows me, and

Sammy too, I guess.

Gerry is on his fourth plate of chicken wings when Kyle comes in with Jess, which is weird. She's supposed to be babysitting. But whatever. Kyle comes over to the drink station where I'm mopping up a puddle of Mountain Dew.

"Hey, babe." Kyle kisses me quick. His five-o'clock shadow is scratchy and he smells like chlorine and old beer. He's got a pretty bad sunburn on his nose and forehead. He's probably gonna peel. Gross.

"Oh my god, is that the guy?" Jess bobs her head in Gerry's direction. She's doing something different and stupid with her bangs. Are those my blue flip flops with the sequins?

"Jesus, Heath, you weren't kidding about that guy." Kyle looks from Gerry to Jess and then at me. "He's disgusting." I'm glad he never met Mom.

Jess laughs and snaps her gum. "What time are you getting out?" She pokes at the mini yellow sponge cakes on the dessert buffet. "We're gonna go down to the Switz."

"I can't leave until the last customer goes."

"That could be a month," Kyle says. Jess laughs her donkey

laugh and touches his arm. Kyle has a sweet tattoo of barbed wire that wraps all the way around his bicep, except for the underside of his arm. He tells people he's gonna get it finished one day, but I was there when he was getting it done and he totally cried and begged the tattoo guy to stop.

"How many chicken wings has he had?"

Jess says it loud enough that Gerry hears. He looks up from the plates in front of him, littered with tiny broken bones. There's grease on his cheeks, shiny in the light from the overhead fluorescents. He waves to me to come over.

"Ooh, watch out, Kyle. I think this guy's got a thing for Heather."

I walk over and give Gerry my best smile. I totally love my new teeth whitener. "What's up?" This might be the first time I've ever spoken directly to Gerry. I mean, face to face.

"Could you bring my check, please?"

"Eileen just went on break. She can bring it when she gets back."

Gerry wipes his mouth with the corner of his napkin, which is dark with grease. It's delicate, the way he does it, like his hand isn't the size of a baseball mitt. Mom was like that, too—huge but gentle. Like they need to be soft to the world because otherwise they might break it. "I need to leave now. I'm not feeling well."

I look back over my shoulder to see if I can catch Eileen before she goes out for a smoke, and I see Jess totally flirting with Kyle. Like, her hand is on the back of his neck. What is it with people? You think you know them and then all of the sudden they turn out to be a total skank.

Gerry grabs my arm. His hand is hot, too hot, and clammy. It's like a hot-water bottle on my skin.

"Okay, I'll get your check, just give me a sec—"

I look down, and Gerry's face is way too red. His eyes, almost lost behind the fat mounds of his cheeks, bulge. He lets go of my arm and his giant fist smashes onto the table. Silverware rattles. The salt shaker falls to the floor and rolls past my feet.

Jess and Kyle have stopped groping each other long enough to come over to see what's going on.

"Oh my God, is he having a heart attack?" Jess says. She backs away from the booth.

I look over at Kyle, and he's really pale. The splotches of

sunburn on his nose and forehead make him look like he's got some kind of tropical disease. Picked up in Puerto Rico for all I know. "We should go," he says.

It's late but it's not late enough that we should be the only people there, but we are. Eileen is out back smoking, who knows where Stan and Jan are, and I'm the only busser who has to stay past eight. There isn't even another customer in the place. So much for, "Is there a doctor in the house?"

Gerry starts to slide under the booth, but the chair catches on the carpet and he ends up kind of wedged between it and the table. He makes a noise that sounds like "garg" and then his eyes roll back in his head.

I went to first aid training every Saturday morning for weeks at the YMCA. I know CPR and mouth-to-mouth and the Heimlich, too. I know that I have to get Gerry on the floor and then I can get him breathing again. I shout at Kyle to help me, but he just stands there with his hands shoved in the pockets of his khakis.

"I'll call 911," he says. He dials while I pull the chair out from under Gerry. I'm totally skinny, so it takes every bit of strength I have, but finally Gerry slumps down onto the floor. His sneakers thunk against the tile under the booth.

I was getting ready for prom when Mom died. She choked on some pizza bites; I was upstairs getting dressed and Sammy was watching TV and didn't hear the chair knock into the stove. By the time I came downstairs to have Mom help zip up my dress, she was already purple.

Gerry's not purple. Not yet.

I lace my fingers together and press my hands, palm down, between his breasts. Seriously, he has breasts, bigger than mine. My hands sink into his soft flesh. Gross. Was Mom this soft and fleshy?

"Oh my god, are you going to give him mouth-to-mouth?"

"Yes, Jess." I lean over and put my lips right on Gerry's. Swear to God I can taste Super Fire Hot Sauce. I breathe as much breath into Gerry as I can. I think I see his chest inflate a little. I shift my weight and start pressing on Gerry's chest again. I count with my eyes closed. When I open them, I see my blue sequined flip flops standing close to Kyle's busted old deck shoes.

"That is so gross," Jess says.

"Jesus, I think she's saving his life," Kyle says.

"Still, gross."

"Well, yeah." They laugh. They laugh!

Press, press, press on the chest and then back to the mouth. My cheeks are covered in chicken wing grease and my arms feel like lead.

"They're here, they're here!"

It's Eileen, and she's got paramedics with her. I'm not sure, but I think the cute one with the short red hair is the same guy who came to the house when Mom died. I wonder if he remembers me. I think his name is Steve. I wipe the grease off my mouth with the back of my hand and smile at him.

There's a lot of shouting then, and some pushing, and the smell of latex gloves. I find Kyle, who's back over by the soda machine. Jess has her face pressed against his tattoo.

"I can't even look, I can't believe you kissed that guy!"

"I didn't kiss him, you moron."

"Might as well have," Kyle says. He won't look me in the eye.

We watch as Steve and the other medic try to put Gerry on a stretcher. They've got an oxygen mask on him, and his big chest goes up and down, up and down. They can't even strap him down; he's too big. They couldn't strap Mom down, either.

I take off my apron and toss it onto the buffet, where it lands in the Jell-O. I think about mountains of guacamole, about the sweet syrupy taste of a non-diet Coke, about Super Fire Hot Sauce on fatty chicken wings.

"Where're you going?" Kyle asks.

"With Gerry."

Jess says, "Gross."

# Fatherhood

Bo is eating lunch when Missy calls to tell him she's pregnant. She cries when she tells him that she bought three different tests just to be sure. He chews his baloney on white and wonders if she's crying because she's happy or sad.

After work, his buddies take him to The Tavern and buy him tequila shooters to celebrate the news. He stumbles to bed at 1:24 with one sock on and one sock off. Missy is curled up on her side of the bed, hands tucked under the pillow, snoring.

In the morning, he wakes up when she turns on the hair dryer. She's upside down, brushing the curls out of her blond hair with hard, fast strokes. She wears her new scrubs, the pink ones with butterflies. When she stands up and looks at him in the mirror, he pretends to be asleep.

\*\*\*

Missy is sick all through the first three months. Bo sleeps through most of the morning sickness, although sometimes the retching wakes him. Then he turns over and puts his back to the bathroom door. Bo works the 3-11 shift at the Wal-Mart. He is the warehouse supervisor, and has half a dozen boys and one girl who report to him. Missy works four twelve-hour shifts at the hospital; she is a nurse in the operating room. If she isn't too tired, on her nights off she drives over to Wal-Mart and brings Bo tuna casserole or sloppy joes for dinner. By the end of her third month, she is already starting to waddle when she crosses the stained gray warehouse floor, Tupperware and a stack of napkins in a cloth bag in her hand.

Bo was twenty-four when he met Missy at his cousin's wedding. Missy was a sorority sister of the bride, a skinny red-headed girl from New Jersey. Missy grew up in Boston, and moved to Newark with her mom when her parents split up. At the end of the night, after he finished a six-pack of beer for courage, Bo asked Missy to dance. He thought Missy was beautiful, with her long blond hair, her tiny waist, the aqua dress with the matching high heels. She gave him her telephone number, and a week later he drove to Newark and they met in front of a movie theater to see a showing of *Rear Window* and *Psycho*. It was a week before Halloween.

Bo takes a day off work to go with Missy to the doctor to find out if the baby will be a boy or a girl. On the way, as they sit at the light at Oak and Elm and Bo smells the grease from the McDonald's and the curry from the Indian Jewel Buffet next to it, Missy says Kim suggested a beautiful name for a little girl: Mei. Kim is Missy's new friend; she is the wife of Dr. Tong, the hotshot doctor recruited by the hospital to run the OR. Kim Tong is a stay-at-home mom. The Tongs have six-month-old twins.

The doctor spreads gel over Missy's swollen belly and presses the ultrasound device to her skin. On the computer monitor, Bo sees moving black and white shapes that mean nothing to him. The doctor points out the head, two dark shapes that are the eye sockets, the fingers like tiny white twigs. Missy cries and squeezes Bo's hand.

That night, Missy calls Kim and invites the Tongs to dinner. Because it is so last minute, Kim cannot find a babysitter. At six-thirty, the Tongs arrive with two car seats, two diaper bags, and two black-haired little girls with bright blue eyes that match their mother's. Their names are Ethel and Lucy, because Kim loves *I Love Lucy*. She wants to have two boys someday. They will be Fred and Desi.

Missy serves pork chops smothered in cream of mushroom soup over white rice. Her mother calls it "pork chop slop," and they eat it once a week. Missy fills up their wooden salad bowls with iceberg lettuce, carrots, and radishes she has carved to look like roses.

Throughout dinner, Dr. Tong and Missy talk about the hospital. Dr. Tong is used to a busy OR, gun shot wounds and overdoses. But he is happier now, removing gallbladders and the occasional kidney, nothing out of the ordinary or too difficult. Kim feeds Ethel and then Lucy. Bo can tell them apart because Ethel has a pink ribbon in her hair and Lucy has a yellow ribbon.

After dinner, Dr. Tong offers to help Missy with the dishes (they don't have a dishwasher yet, although Missy's mother has offered to pay for one if they get married in a church). Missy sends Bo into the living room with Kim. The babies roll around on the carpet and drool on each other. Their hair is so black it looks purple in the light from the lamp on the end table. Kim coos to them and says a few words in Chinese that her husband must have taught her. The babies look up at her and smile.

After they'd dated for two years, Missy started asking Bo for a commitment. She wanted a diamond ring, a big wedding, and a house in town (they were living in a double-wide on a corner of his dad's land six miles out of town). Bo had already been saving money for a ring, and on Missy's birthday, September 20, he left the warehouse with $1,600 in his pocket and walked up to the jewelry counter. Janine Duggan, who had been Bo's date to the junior prom, helped him pick out a 1/4 carat ring, gold with emerald chips on the sides. Janine asked him twice if he wanted the matching wedding band, but he said he'd get that later.

A month after the ultrasound, Missy and Dr. Tong travel to a medical conference in Tucson. Missy calls Bo from the hotel, where she has a suite and a fluffy white bathrobe and room service. She will get a pregnancy massage in the morning.

She is gone for three days. On the second day, he gets a phone call from Kim, inviting him to dinner. It is his night off, so he calls her back and says yes.

Kim meets him at the door of the huge brick house wearing a blue apron and carrying Lucy (or maybe Ethel) on her hip.

"Do you know anything about twice-baked potatoes?" she asks.

Bo doesn't, but she puts him to work anyway, adding butter and sour cream to the already mashed potatoes. She teaches him to squeeze the pastry tube gently, so the potato jackets fill up with pretty scallops of white. He sprinkles paprika on each one before Kim puts them in the oven to bake a second time.

"How long until you get married?" Kim asks when they sit down to their salads—spinach and radishes and baby carrots, which Bo pushes to the side of his plate. "With the baby on the way, it seems like a good time, right?"

Kim is not as pretty as Missy, but softer. She smells like lavender and baby powder. Bo caught a whiff when she leaned over him to put the stuffed chicken breasts on the table. She is short and a little chubby (Missy says Kim was skinny before the babies). Her hair is cut very short. It reminds him of Mr. Spock from the old *Star Trek* TV show. Kim wears tiny pearl earrings and a matching necklace. The babies reach for the necklace whenever she holds them.

During dinner, the babies sleep in a plastic and nylon playpen that Kim puts in a corner of the dining room.

"Soon," Bo says in answer to the question that eventually everyone asks him. "We're gonna get married soon."

He doesn't mind the idea of marriage—his own mom and dad have been married for almost forty years, and his Papa and Gram Buck were together sixty-some years when Papa got crushed by the back loader.

"A nice church wedding?" Kim asks, and puts another twice-baked potato on his plate. The scalloped edges are brown and crusty but the inside potatoes melt on his tongue. "A nice church wedding before the baby comes?"

"Yes," Bo says.

The next day at work, he walks over to Jewelry and has Janine Duggan help him pick out a wedding band for Missy. The afternoon after that, he takes off work so he can pick Missy up at the airport. Dr. Tong is staying in Arizona for another two days to learn a new procedure.

Bo finds a seat outside the security checkpoint and watches the people who file out of the sliding glass doors. Mostly business people in black or dark gray suits, carrying briefcases and computer bags, and every once in awhile someone who looks like him: a little soft in the belly, in need of a haircut and a shave, wearing Levi's and shit kickers.

It takes him a minute or two to realize it's Missy walking towards him. She is a little tanner and a lot more pregnant than she was when she left.

"I missed you," he says, hugging her close and feeling her warm cheek pressed up against his.

"It was so great," she says, handing him her bag. "The pregnancy massage was the best thing that's ever been done to me, I swear. And Dr. Tong took me to this unbelievable steak house—you would have loved it—where you buy everything separate and just a little filet was fifty dollars!"

They are at the baggage carousel now, waiting for Missy's green suitcase to come through the plastic flaps. Missy talks on and on about Tucson: the weather, the hotel, the limo that took them from and back to the airport, getting bumped up to first class on the flight home from Atlanta, and how she'd been sad not to be able to drink the free champagne.

"They give you a choice of meals—not just peanuts like in coach—and I watched a movie, and the stewardess got me a hot towel for my hands and face."

Bo has never been on an airplane.

\*\*\*

When Missy is two months from her due date, they stand in front of Justice Millard. Kim and Dr. Tong are there, and so are Bo's friends, Mike and Charlie. The ring from Wal-Mart is in Charlie's pocket. Missy's parents will be in town in the morning; the reception will be at the Elks tomorrow afternoon.

Justice Millard asks if Missy does and she says yes. Justice Millard asks Bo if he does—and just like in a made-for-TV movie, Missy faints, collapsing to the tiled courthouse floor, crushing her bouquet of pink roses.

The next time Bo sees her, Missy is propped up in a hospital bed with monitors stuck to her bare belly. Machines hum and beep around her. Dr. Murphy comes in carrying a silver clipboard.

"Bed rest until the baby comes," he says. Missy starts to cry. Bo holds her left hand; Dr Murphy pats her right. "You'll both be fine."

\*\*\*

Kim comes to visit every afternoon. Her girls crawl around the living room and chew on the remote control. Twice she asks Bo to help her change diapers. "You have never done this before?" she asks the first time he pricks his finger with the diaper pin. He is glad that Missy has decided to use disposable diapers.

"You want to wait to get married now?" Kim asks Missy a week after the attempted wedding. Missy cries a lot of the time now, and Kim hands her a Kleenex.

"I want to stand up when he says 'you may now kiss the bride,'" Missy says. Kim hands Ethel (or Lucy) to Bo and shoos him out of the room.

He tries to listen from the other side of the door, but Lucy (or Ethel) starts to fuss, so he carries her out to the kitchen where her sister is sleeping in her car seat. Bo gives the awake baby a bottle and sits with her in the afternoon sunlight in front of the sliding glass door.

\*\*\*

Dr. Tong and Kim bring dinner almost every night. It's usually something with chicken or fish, but sometimes Kim calls in the morning to see if Missy likes lasagna or pot roast. On a Friday night about a month before Missy's due date, she calls to see if Missy is willing to try something called "baba ganoosh." Missy is napping in front of the television. Bo says he's already made plans to pick up pizza and wings. Kim agrees to just bring something for dessert.

Kim arrives right at six. Dr. Tong is stuck at the hospital, waiting on x-rays of a boy who fell on a piece of rebar. He should be only a few more minutes.

"Isn't she looking so good?" Kim asks when Bo takes her to the guest bedroom where Missy has decided to stay for awhile. First it was their bedroom, and then the living room. When Bo carries her to the back of the trailer (he insisted), she cries and says, "I just need a change of scene, honey." The first night she moved out of their bedroom he felt strange, lonely and almost afraid. Now he stretches his legs and arms as far as they will go, sleeping on the white sheets like a kid making a snow angel.

"I feel good today," Missy says. She pats her enormous tummy and smiles up at Kim and Bo. "How long 'til the pizza's here?"

Bo tips the delivery boy two dollars. They eat the pizza and wings in the back bedroom, Bo and Kim sitting Indian-style on the carpet. Dr. Tong called to say he'd be longer than expected, to eat without him, but save him a slice or two. Ethel (Bo is sure of it—Kim has cut Ethel's hair short to match her own, but left Lucy's longer) likes chicken wings, but her sister doesn't.

"You going to be in for the delivery?" Kim asks Bo when they are at the kitchen sink, rinsing off cheesy plates. "Not such a big deal, unless Missy needs a C-section, right?"

Missy is determined to have a natural birth. She makes Bo attend the childbirth classes at the hospital even though she can't go because of the bed rest Dr. Murphy has insisted on. Bo is not the only single parent there, but he is the only single man.

Dr. Tong arrives at the house around eight. Lucy and Ethel are sound asleep in their car seats. Kim knits a blanket for the new baby while she and Bo watch the Red Sox on TV in the living room.

"I'll just check on the patient before I eat," Dr. Tong says, and heads for the back bedroom. While he's gone, Bo reheats the leftover pizza in the oven. They ate all the wings.

*** 

The first time Bo thought Dr. Tong was gay was the night of the reception welcoming him to the hospital. It was a dinner at the fancy new place on the lake. Missy wore a white flowered dress—Bo remembered it because she had paid a fortune for it a year before and had never worn it—and he wore his navy suit jacket and dress pants.

It was a long night, and Bo had been very glad to see Charlie there, his best friend. Charlie had just started dating a girl who was working in the hospital gift shop. Bo and Charlie were in the restaurant bar, drinking Coors Light, when Dr. Tong walked up to where they were standing and called the bartender over.

"White wine for my wife," Dr. Tong said. His voice was high-pitched and nasally. Bo looked at the doctor's hands—white and soft-looking. His own were dry and callused.

"And for you?" the bartender asked.

"Shirley Temple," Dr. Tong said. Charlie elbowed Bo.

They watched as the doctor walked away with the drinks. He took the maraschino cherry out of his Shirley Temple and chewed it as he left.

"He popped that cherry, huh?" Bo said.

Charlie laughed and slapped Bo's shoulder. "That fairy ain't never popped a cherry in his life."

Bo told Charlie he was a poet and didn't know it, and then they finished their beers and went into the other room to see what was for dessert.

***

On a Tuesday night about three weeks before Missy is due, Bo stands out back of the loading docks with some of his crew, watching the boys take a smoke break. When he hears his name over the loudspeaker, he is sure Missy has gone into labor. He picks up Line 2 but it is not Missy, it's Kim.

"You want to meet me and the girls for dinner?" she asks. "My husband is working late, and Missy's cousin is with her, right?"

Bo agrees to meet Kim at The Tavern on his lunch break at 7:30.

It's almost empty when he gets there—just a few old girls playing euchre in the back, and Tom Breitling and his boys eating fried chicken at the bar. Bo sits down next to Kim because Lucy and Ethel are taking up the other bench. The girls are asleep, pacifiers in their mouths, wearing pink overalls.

"I ordered, okay? Fish for me and a burger for you?"

Over the food, Kim talks about Dr. Tong's plans to open his own practice in the next five years. He will ask Missy to leave the hospital with him and be his nurse. Is Bo okay with that? Sure, if the money is right.

Kim asks, "Are you always going to work at night? Missy will get very lonely—sad—alone with just the baby, you know?"

Bo looks over at Ethel and Lucy. Lucy's hair is in a ponytail on top of her hand. He starts to say something about a promotion his boss mentioned (day shift plus a big salary bump if Bo spends six months on 11-7), but then Kim's hand is in his lap. He looks down and sees her shiny pink fingernails with the white tips, the emerald and sapphire ring that Missy always reminds Bo that she loves. Kim's hand just rests there near his knee for a few minutes, and then it starts to creep closer to his crotch.

He lets her rub him for a few minutes until he has a huge erection.

"Come home with us, okay?" Kim asks. One of the babies makes a gurgling sound.

"I can't," Bo says. He pulls out his wallet and takes his time getting the money out—long enough so that his hard-on mostly goes away. He leaves a really good tip and walks away without making eye contact with Kim.

***

Bo has never cheated, but he has been cheated on. Once, in high school. Janine Duggan went to the prom with Bo, but she left with Stu Hansen. Bo left the dance early and got shit-faced drunk with Mike and Charlie down at the boat launch.

He finishes his shift and drives home. There is a wreck on Route 14, blocking both sides of the road, and he is stuck for the better part of an hour. He thinks about calling Missy but doesn't want to wake her.

He fiddles with the radio for awhile and settles on a country station out of Watkins Glen. The DJ plays Trisha Yearwood, Missy's favorite. The song is "Walkaway Joe."

The second time Bo met Dr. Tong was at Kim's baby shower, which was the first baby shower Bo had ever been to. He was one of six men—all the rest were doctors from the hospital. They kept to themselves in a corner of the room, away from the wrapping paper and ribbons, close to the finger sandwiches and punch.

Dr. Tong sat next to Kim as she unwrapped two of everything: boxes of diapers, tiny yellow hats, leather shoes, teddy bears. After the gifts were all opened, the women began cutting and handing out pieces of coconut cake. Dr. Tong asked the men if they wanted to see the new pool. They did.

He walked with little steps, delicate almost, like he was tip-toeing. A queer for sure, Bo thought, but he didn't think the other doctors seemed to notice or mind.

When they were admiring the wooden deck and fence around the new pool, Dr. Tong tip-toed over to Bo and stuck out his hand.

Bo shook it; it was like shaking hands with a woman—weak and moist. Bo wondered for the first time if Dr. Tong was really the father of Kim's babies. Maybe they got her pregnant just to keep up the show. But what did Kim get out of it? A new pool, babies she could dress up, a BMW ragtop.

Bo towered over Dr. Tong. He was a big guy—husky, his mom still called him—and the doctor barely came up to his breast bone.

"Missy is an amazing nurse," Dr. Tong said in his sing-song voice. "The hospital is very lucky to have her." Bo thanked him. "I hope that you'll continue to support her in her career."

Bo told Dr. Tong that he always supported Missy in everything. Dr. Tong patted Bo's arm in a motherly way and walked back to the house.

\*\*\*

Two days after their dinner at The Tavern, Bo and Kim meet at the grocery store. He is buying grape soda and peanut butter cookies for Missy. Kim is ordering a cake for Ethel and Lucy's first birthday party, which is a month away.

"Everything is okay with us?" she asks. Bo nods his head. Kim's fingernails are red. Her hair needs a trim. "Do you want steak or chicken for dinner tonight?" It occurs to Bo that to the Tongs, he and Missy are probably poor.

"Missy wants take-out from The Chicken Coop," Bo says. It is a lie, but Bo knows that Kim doesn't like the greasy fried chicken and deep-fried corn fritters.

"Okay. Tomorrow then?" It's Kim's turn at the bakery counter, so Bo slips away when she turns to talk to the girl behind the register.

***

That night, Missy's water breaks. Bo calls Dr. Murphy, who delivered Bo and his sister. Dr. Murphy tells Bo to get the overnight bag and meet him at the emergency room.

She is in labor for the entire night. Bo calls her mother, feeds Missy ice chips, walks her up and down the empty hospital hallways.

His mom shows up around 5:30, curlers still in her hair. At seven, Kim appears. She's left the girls home with Dr. Tong, whose shift doesn't start until noon.

At 10:10 they hand Bo a green gown and mask. He has never been in an operating room before. It is much brighter than he thought it would be. He stands near Missy's head and holds her hand. She squeezes hard with every contraction.

"No drugs!" she says. Her teeth are clenched and her fingernails dig half moons into Bo's skin. "I don't want it!"

Bo breathes with her: first long, deep inhales, then rapid exhales, hoo hoo hoo hoo. She pushes and screams, and then Dr. Murphy says, "It's a girl!" He holds up a bloody little mess, all arms and legs, and then Bo's daughter announces herself to the world. Bo barely gets a look at her before a nurse takes her away.

"We'll get her cleaned up and then you can hold her," the nurse says.

Missy wipes snot and tears off her face. "Go tell Mom she's here," she says. She pushes weakly at Bo's arm. "Go on, you can come right back."

Bo walks past the nurse who is cleaning up his daughter, his baby girl. He sees her tiny feet. She cries again, and Bo wants very much to see her face.

"Go on," Missy says again.

*** 

People are everywhere—his mom and dad, his sister Jessica and a bunch of her friends, Charlie and Mike. Half an hour after the baby is born, Missy's family arrives. Bo brings them one by one into the room where Missy is resting. The baby has a little pink hat, is wrapped in a pink blanket. Her little face is pressed against Missy's chest.

Kim is there all afternoon and into the evening, bringing him coffee and donuts, making phone calls from a list Missy has given her. At seven o'clock, she disappears and comes back with pizza. At eight thirty, when visiting hours end, she stands on tip-toes and kisses Bo on the mouth. He looks around to see who has noticed, but they are all alone in the waiting area. He hears the squeak of shoes from the nurses station down the hall.

"You call me later, okay?" she asks. Bo tells her he's just going to run home to get some sleep, he won't need anything from her. Kim laughs, "You'll call me."

\*\*\*

Bo doesn't have a chance to hold the baby. Every time he tries, she is in someone else's arms. And then, in a quiet moment when it is just the three of them, Missy looks from the baby, who is nursing, to Bo and says, "Let's get married right now."

Justice Millard is sent for. Charlie gets the rings. Within an hour, Bo and Missy are married. Both Kim and Missy cry when the justice says, "I now pronounce you man and wife."

Before she falls asleep, Missy tells Bo that she has decided to name the baby Jasmine. "You pick the middle name," she says.

"I'll sleep on it."

He walks down the hall to the nursery. Dr. Tong is standing in front of the window, looking at the babies. He looks very unhappy.

"Will they let me go in and hold her?" Bo asks.

Dr. Tong shakes his head like he is coming out of a trance. "Of course." He holds the door open for Bo. "See you tomorrow," he says.

Jasmine is tiny, just an ounce over six pounds. Her hair is thick, shiny, jet black. Her eyes are shaped like almonds and her eyelids are not creased like Bo's. He looks down at his left hand, at the new gold band on his finger.

He will love Jasmine. He will raise her as his own. He will ignore the whispers and stares of his friends. He will come up with a funny answer to the "What country is she from?" questions he will get from strangers at the grocery store, on line at the movies. He will teach her to ride a bike, to build a bird house, to dance. He will take her to piano lessons, swimming meets, the mall. He will protect her from bee stings and skinned knees, mean girlfriends and abusive boyfriends. He will teach her to read and to write and to be faithful to the people she loves.

Bo looks down at the baby sleeping in his arms and thinks of Kim's hand in his lap under the table.

# Jackpot

Mount Rushmore isn't open at night. Sherri pulls up in front of the park entrance at just after one in the morning. She shifts the van into park and turns off the radio. She cracks her knuckles and then squeezes her hands into stiff fists. Her fingers are swollen from gripping the steering wheel.

She closes her eyes, sees her family as she left them back at the hotel: Bill and the boys, asleep on the pull-out sofa in the flickering light of the Rockies game. Seth wears a plastic glow-in-the-dark necklace on his head like a crown; it colors his blond hair a sickly purple. Jack's bare feet are pressed into Bill's back. Bill's mouth is open, jaw slack, one hand loosely curled around Jack's wrist. On the coffee table pushed up under the window are three half-empty milkshakes, two vanilla, one strawberry, and a plate of limp French fries.

She'd only had three beers at dinner, but Bill had insisted on driving home from the restaurant, so when she decided to go out for a drive, she couldn't find the van. The parking lot was a flood of light that teased the dull pain she'd been feeling all day into a full-blown headache. She picked her way from shadow to shadow, avoided the cluster of smokers crowded around a propped open side door. She finally found the van parked at the back of the hotel, as far from their room as possible, of course, and wedged in so close to a gold Cadillac that she had to climb in from the passenger side.

It had been Bill's idea to come to South Dakota. Their last vacation as a family should be special, he'd said. Sherri had suggested Disney, maybe Sea World. Something that would really stimulate the boys. But Bill said the Black Hills would be educational. In the fall, the boys would be the only ones in their class with stories about gun fights and bison and prairie dogs. Sherri said they wouldn't remember any stories to share with their classmates, which led to another argument about Sherri's lack of faith in their children. In the end, Bill had worn her down, and they'd loaded up the van and driven north.

There were plenty of decent hotels in downtown Deadwood, but Bill had found Gulches of Fun online and mentioned it to the boys before discussing it with Sherri. Seth and Jack were mesmerized by words they didn't understand: go karts, miniature golf, skee ball. Slot machines right in the hotel. Breakfast buffet, room service, indoor pool. They'd been in Deadwood three days and had only left the hotel once, for dinner at the Double D Bar & Grill. No hike up to Mount Moriah Cemetery to see Wild Bill Hickok's grave, no afternoon escape from the heat in the cool caverns of Wind Cave over in Hot Springs, no pictures of the boys waving miniature stars and stripes with the presidents looking over their shoulders.

That morning, before the boys woke, Sherri walked into the bathroom to suggest to her husband, again, that they drive to Keystone.

"They're having fun," Bill said. He crunched ice between his front teeth, swallowed the shards. "We can go to Rushmore tomorrow."

"We could walk up to the cemetery," Sherri said. She flapped a brochure in his direction. He looked at it, then back at Sherri.

"It's hot."

"If we go early, we can beat the heat."

"It's going to be ninety. The boys want to swim." He brushed his graying hair, rough strokes that tugged the skin at his temples.

Sherri squeezed toothpaste. "You don't know what they want." She brushed.

Bill poured aftershave into his hands, clapped, slapped his cheeks and neck. "What's that supposed to mean?"

Sherri spit. "You wanted to come here for you. Don't pretend this is for the boys. They don't want to sit in a hotel all day."

It is the same argument they have had countless times before. The argument they started having even before the boys were born.

Bill leaned close to the mirror, picked at a scab on his chin. "They have fun in the pool. Seth likes to swim."

"He can't swim."

"He can float. We'll get him some of those arm floats."

"He'll drown."

"Jesus, Sherri," Bill said. He met the reflection of her eyes. "He's not going to drown."

This was the part in the argument where he would accuse her of wanting something terrible to happen, to make it easier for her. And then it would be her turn to deny such thoughts, even though they wormed their way farther into her heart each day.

"Da?"

They turned; Jack stood in the doorway, his thumb in his mouth and his pull-up diaper around his ankles.

The fourth day in Deadwood: roulette wheels, sunburns, steamed hot dogs and salt and vinegar potato chips. In the afternoon, a thunderstorm. Sherri thumbed a paperback. The boys took a nap. Bill lost two hundred dollars at the poker table. Dinner at the Double D, a doggie bag for Seth's leftover French fries and Styrofoam cups for milkshakes. Sherri had finished Jack's bacon cheeseburger and Bill's Heinekens. She didn't believe in leftovers.

\*\*\*

Sherri thinks she's scraped the rear bumper of the Cadillac as she backs out of the parking space. To be sure, she puts the transmission into drive and pulls forward until she hears the satisfying crunch of the van's front bumper meeting the Caddy's rear end. According to the Florida license plate, the gold boat belongs to GR8GRPA.

Her clothes are still in the room, but she has her purse, her driver's license, and a few hundred dollars in cash. Bill had taken the debit card out of her wallet; he needed more money to use in the casino, and hadn't remembered to give it back. She has enough money to get back to Denver, at least. But first: Mount Rushmore.

Which is closed. There's no moon, and she can only see the dark edges of the presidents' heads against the black sky.

There's a map in the glove box, worn thin at the folded edges. Van idling, Sherri sits hunched over the map. Her finger traces the squiggly line that will take her from Keystone to points south. Home to Denver, to suitcases and the cardboard boxes she's been stashing in the basement, waiting to be filled.

She puts the van in gear and pulls out onto the smooth surface of Route 385. It's too dark to drive fast, the road too curvy for cruise control. She cranks the window down to hear the chattering of prairie dogs, the low, mournful howl of a coyote.

***

"What are you going to tell the boys?" she asked Bill, the cloudless morning a month ago when she'd told him she wanted a divorce. The boys always listened better when Bill talked; it would be better if the news came from him.

"I haven't decided yet."

Typical Bill. Seven thirty at night, the boys crying on the couch, Sherri just home from another exhausting day at the store, her stomach rumbling. What's for dinner? I haven't decided yet. Small things like dinner; big things like deformed fetuses. There's something wrong with one of your twins, Mr. and Mrs. Harrell. He has Down Syndrome. Sherri felt the chair underneath her but didn't recall deciding to sit down. Just one? The other is fine? From what we can tell, just one. We will run more tests to be sure. But the odds of having identical twins with Down Syndrome are approximately one in a million. Oh, god, Bill, what are we going to do? I haven't decided yet.

Sherri is not a gambler, but Bill is an addict.

The odds were with them; Bill assured her they could deal with one disabled child. And so the damaged twin was not aborted. Months of late-night meals of frozen pizza and warm diet soda. Working until her due date, and then past. Belly, feet swollen.

Damaged twin not aborted, but born. And then the horror, the cold fist that gripped her heart and squeezed, as Bill held the second boy out to her, the one who was supposed to be fine. Identical twins. Identical. Look, Bill said. They're one in a million, our boys.

***

Not that she doesn't love Seth and Jack. It's just a lot to ask of her—of anyone—to raise two special needs children, boys who will need around-the-clock care for the rest of their lives, raised by a stay-at-home father more interested in slot machines and scratch tickets than keeping his family happy and fed. When she said, "I want a divorce," he had been watching the news for that night's quick pick numbers and so she said it again to make sure he'd heard.

"Well," he had finally replied. "I'm not surprised." She was relieved and heartbroken.

"I still want to see the boys."

"See them?"

She swallowed, pushed the words up through the tight tunnel of her throat. "I don't want custody."

"You're their mother." Bill crumpled the quick pick ticket and tossed it onto the coffee table.

"I didn't want them," she said. "And I don't want to do this anymore." She could only look at the carpet.

*\*\*\**

Sherri steers the van along the silent, winding roads of southwest South Dakota. The casinos are dark; Mount Rushmore is gated until morning. There is nothing to do but drive.

And worry about the boys. Seth is outgoing, brave and willing to jump off the top step of the back porch, or try a fish taco, as long as his daddy is there. He follows Bill around the yard, pushing the plastic lawnmower that spits bubbles out the back, hooting back at the birds. Jack prefers to be in the kitchen with Sherri, thumb in his mouth, a coloring book open on the table in front of him. Although they are seven, neither of the boys can read yet, but Seth is getting close. He recognizes pictures of cows, dogs, butterflies. Jack uses books to build ramps for his Matchbox cars.

Seth will be okay; he is daddy's little boy. Bill saves all his patience for Seth. But who will take Jack for walks around the neighborhood after dinner when Sherri is gone? Bill and Seth spend evenings on the couch watching Sesame Street. Who will show

Jack again how to tie his shoes? Seth just lets Bill do it—he can't be bothered, there are too many things to look at, too many adventures to be had. But Jack wants to learn, even when he gets so frustrated his face turns red and he starts to shake. Who will be patient enough to teach Jack how to throw a football, ride a bicycle, dance with a girl? Seth can already ride a bicycle; he's so much more coordinated than his brother.

But Jack has potential. Jack could be someone special. Maybe Bill will let her take Jack. She said she didn't want them, couldn't handle them, but if she only had Jack, maybe she could do it.

\*\*\*

Sherri pulls over to the side of the road and lets her head fall into her hands. She hasn't cried since Seth and Jack were born— since she saw their matching sweet, almond eyes and broad, flat faces. She has been too numb to cry. Two babies, one in a million, two damaged babies because Bill said the odds were good. Even if Jack could learn to tie his shoes and ride a bike and dance with a girl, Sherri will still spend the rest of her life taking care of her son, holding his hand at the grocery store when Jack is twenty, cutting his roast beef when Jack is middle aged and Sherri no longer has teeth to chew her own dinner.

The first word Jack said was "da." But he was looking at Sherri when he said it.

***

"What are you going to do?" Sherri shoved undershirts and elastic-waist shorts into a Spider-Man suitcase for the boys. It is a ten hour drive to Deadwood, so Sherri packed coloring books and crayons, the plastic CD player.

Bill looked at her and said, "About what?"

"About the boys. You can't take care of them alone."

"You aren't giving me much of a choice."

Sherri picked up Jack's pillow, squeezed it. "I know, I'm sorry. But I just can't. I can't live here. I can't deal with this every day." She dropped the pillow back on Jack's bed and began rooting through the boys' dresser for socks. "I didn't want this."

"Want what?"

"Them. Like this."

"The doctors said one of them was going to be okay. I wasn't going to let you kill him. Either of them."

"I didn't mean that."

"What else did you mean?"

A few minutes of silence. Yes, she did want to end the pregnancy. Her lungs had filled with ice water that day.

Sherri said: "I can give you money."

"You're going to give me money. A lot of it." Bill sat down on Seth's bed. His voice was thin when he said: "And the house."

"We shouldn't go on this trip. You can just take the money we would've spent there and use it for the boys."

"This trip is for the boys."

Sherri's jaw clenched. "This trip is so you can blow a thousand dollars on slot machines."

Bill laughed, a sharp, short bark. Sherri held the Spider-Man suitcase out to him. "Put this in the van. I'll get the boys."

\*\*\*

Sherri gets out of the car and walks into the dark. Something small scuttles away from her. There is no moon to see by. She will just walk for awhile, clear her head, clear her lungs. She will breathe.

She steps into a hole, falls, hears the crack of bone before she feels the pain. She cries out, but only the prairie dogs hear her.

She lays on the uneven ground with her arm thrown over her eyes. She breathes irregularly, in large gulps. Her left foot is still in the prairie dog hole; it hurts too much to move. Her phone is in her purse. Her purse is in the van.

A few hundred feet away, at the tree line, something large moves. A branch snaps. Sherri lowers her arm and looks toward the sound. A shape, nearly as big as the van, emerges from the shadow.

"Hello," Sherri says, the word a sigh.

The bison comes closer, its enormous, shaggy head swinging low. It sniffs at Sherri's feet, her left ankle cocked at an unsettling angle. It sniffs at the knees of her jeans. Her hand.

\*\*\*

Bill had taken Seth and Jack into the casino on the bottom floor of Gulches of Fun before dinner at the Double D. Sherri followed, after a quick detour to the bar for a bottle of cold beer. No one under twenty-one was allowed in the casino, but once the manager saw Jack and Seth's matching blank faces, the rules no longer applied. Bill sat at the slot machine with one boy on each knee, letting them take turns pulling the silver arm, feeding nickels into the greedy slot. Sherri stood to the side, gulping the beer, the liquid cold and soothing on her throat.

Then Seth shouted, "Win!" and Jack began to screech. Bill whooped. Sherri turned to see him holding Seth's hands under the river of silver pouring from the machine, the flood of nickels.

***

The bison sniffs at Sherri's jacket. Bill doesn't need her money. Bill has eight dollars in nickels that he will turn into eight hundred dollars at the poker table the next night. Bill has a mother who can move into the spare bedroom. He has friends who will introduce him to their sisters, cousins, coworkers. Someone kind and unselfish who will be patient with the boys and who will teach them both to tie their shoes, to ride their bikes, to dance.

The bison turns its head so that the sharp, stiff horn tugs at Sherri's jacket, runs up the side of her cheek. Sweat pools into the hollow of her throat. If the boys can remember the story to tell it, it will be a good one: My mama got gored to death by a bison. She broke her ankle in a prairie dog hole. She couldn't get up and the bison got her and that's why my mama went away.

Hot, rancid breath floods Sherri's nostrils. She tenses her arms, her legs, her spine. Readies herself for the pull of flesh from bone. Maybe this is better than moving to Tucson or Nashville. This way, she's not a mother who abandoned her sons. This way, she will be remembered for bringing oatmeal cookies to their second grade class, for hanging their macaroni art on the refrigerator, for being a selfless, patient mother. For loving them. This is better, to be taken from them. Sherri closes her eyes. Ready.

The bison grunts and walks off into the dark.

# Three Times Fast

She hasn't thought of the nightmare in years. The last time it had woken her, breathless, her skin slick with sweat, she had been just nine years old. Then her father died, and the nightmare changed.

Now her breath quickens, her forearms marble into gooseflesh. She closes her eyes and takes a step back, directly onto Max's foot.

"Ow! Watch it," he says. He shakes his head and goes back to writing on the coffee-stained pad of paper he keeps tucked in his back pocket.

Caroline looks again, a child's peek, though she resists the urge to cover her eyes with her splayed fingers. It is not just a door, it's the exact door from the nightmare that plagued her as a child, that left her screaming in the milky light of near dawn, terrifying her sister and causing Daphne—as if she needed cause—to wet the bed again. When the nightmares stopped, Caroline forgot the door completely, but now it comes into sharp and immediate focus: the burnt umber rust flakes on the hinges, the weather-beaten wood, splintered and pale gray, the color of driftwood. The knob is the worst of it, copper aged green, embellished with one of those eyeless angel faces that decorate tombstones in neglected cemeteries full of the long dead.

"Breathing is a requirement," Max says.

"What?"

"For life. Breathing. You should try it."

"I'm breathing."

"Jesus, Carrie. The look on your face right now, I mean, it's exactly what people mean when they say 'you look like you've seen a ghost.'" Max snaps a picture and, blissfully, the light momentarily blinds her.

Caroline turns her back on the door, although that is almost worse than facing it. "Let's get out of here. I'm hungry." She isn't, but Max will do whatever she asks if food is involved.

Caroline knows that the breathing she hears behind her, ragged and shallow, is just Max (a pack-a-day smoker), but she bites down on her lower lip to squelch a scream. Copper floods her mouth. It's only five steps across the narrow room from the nightmare door to the green metal door that leads to the tunnels proper, but her feet sink in the wet cement of her terrified childhood, and each step takes approximately a year, one for each year the nightmare came.

When they are safely back in the mailroom—long vacant, a pile of 1996 Yellow Pages rotting in the corner beneath the empty mailboxes—Caroline's heart begins to slow. While Max packs the gear, Caroline risks a look back. Three steps lead down to the tunnels, which split off, left and right, to the main academic buildings on campus. In between is the green door, and behind that green door is the nightmare.

There is nothing to see but a hand-lettered sign, the tape in the corners brittle and yellowed, that reads, "Keep Out. This Means You."

***

When Caroline told her sister that she'd accepted a job as a location researcher for "that show with the hunky ghost-hunting brothers," Daphne hadn't laughed. Instead, she'd pleaded with Caroline not to take the job.

"You were afraid of everything. You were afraid of the moon," Daphne said. "And now you're going to research ghosts?"

"I was a kid!"

"Okay, so now you're fine, right? You don't have any more nightmares, no more waking up screaming? How long since Dad's made an appearance at the foot of your bed?"

Those were the nightmares that came after. When Jack Winter was still alive, Caroline was haunted by the door—a door she was sure she had seen in real life, maybe in the cellar at her grandpa's house, maybe in the dark at the end of the hallway in the library, maybe (this was the worst) at school, in the basement where they had to go for music class and the lights always flickered. Everyone told her it wasn't real, there was no door like that anywhere, but she knew. When Jack finally succumbed to the cancer that had turned him into a walking wraith during Caroline's fourth grade year, he became the nightmare. Daphne didn't remember the door, and Caroline did not remind her.

"That's all over, Daph. For years."

In the end, Caroline promised her sister that she would check in daily, and make an appointment with her therapist, and leave the job if it became too much. The more she researched ghosts, the less often the spectre of Jack Winter visited her dreams. The daily calls became weekly, and the therapist appointment was cancelled. Caroline made fast friends with Max, the location scout, as well as the girls who did hair and makeup. She moved into a bigger apartment and adopted a cat and started seeing a man she met at one of Max's barbecues: Dan, a financial advisor.

And then the script about the college came across her desk. They wanted something that looked classic New England, haunted, and she knew the perfect location. Bradford had been shuttered for a decade; ivy grew over the doors, books lined the shelves in the library, white linen tablecloths rotted on the round tables in the dining hall. It was as if they had turned out the lights, locked the doors, and never looked back.

And there were tunnels, as requested.

***

Max plucks the last handful of fries from the cardboard sleeve and dunks them in his milkshake. Chocolate dribbles into his beard.

"You are raising the bar, girl," Max says. "I mean, that place is perfect."

"Good," Caroline says. Her burger is still in its paper wrapper.

"Are you okay?" He puts his hand on top of hers. "What's wrong?"

She runs her tongue along the ridge on her lip where her teeth broke the skin. "That door," she says. "The one with the weird knob."

Max nods, flipping pages in his notebook. A smear of grease smudges the words. He's drawn a sketch of the door, hasty but accurate, and Caroline shivers. "Pretty creepy, right?"

She wants to tell Max about the nightmare, and how it is, somehow, the exact same door. She wants to tell him how, in the childhood dream, she stands in front of it, not moving, barely even breathing, and she cannot leave—she is *not allowed* to leave—until she knocks on that door, three times fast. She is frozen—five, six, eight years old—frozen to the dirt floor, paralyzed. She cannot move and she cannot leave, and she and the door face each other and wait, it creaking—almost breathing—and settling into the earth;

she trembling, shivering in her thin nightgown, and desperately trying to not wet her pants. She knows that she must knock on the door three times fast, but she also knows, in the deepest part of her dreaming brain, that when she does, something will answer. Something big and terrible. Something with teeth. She wants to tell Max that, finally, because she has to pee so very much, she reaches out with one clenched fist and, her mouth frozen in a rictus of fear, feels her knuckles touch the splintered wood. And then she wakes up, shrieking.

But she can't say any of this to Max. In the overheated dining room, under the fluorescent lights, her throat closes and the most she can manage is, "I don't like it."

"Tomorrow when we meet the guy, we'll see if he can let us in."

"In?"

Max crumples the cardboard and waxy paper on his tray and lets out a quiet belch. "In the door. Don't you want to see what's inside?"

***

Caroline picks up coffee on her way to the campus in the

morning. Her pockets are stuffed with cream and sugar, because she doesn't know how Mr. Favell likes it. She and Max both take it black.

Mr. Favell, the town historian, does not drink coffee. He is small, with a pointy nose and a scarf wrapped tight around his throat, although it is a warm day for late October. He ushers them down past the mailroom and into the tunnels, lecturing on the history of the school, admonishing them to watch where they step and to not touch the walls, which are covered with dated graffiti.

"How are we gonna shoot down here if we can't touch anything?" Max says.

Favell shines his flashlight down the left-hand tunnel, then the right. He will take them down each branch in turn, lead them in to the long-shuttered buildings where the tunnels dead end. But first, the beam of light lands on the green door.

"This room," he says, "was used to store things."

"Things," Caroline repeats. She clenches her fists in rhythm to her heartbeat, which is steady and slow. The night before, she had finally spoken aloud about the nightmare door, confessing the story to Dan after downing a bottle of wine. He put his arms around her while she cried, and then they laughed, finally, at how sure she'd been that she was going to pee her pants, and how each dawn it was

Daphne who ended up wetting the bed. Caroline thinks now, as she watches the historian pull a jangle of keys from his coat pocket, that she would like to introduce Dan to her sister.

"Things. Yes. An assortment of things," Favell says. He pushes open the green door and there is it, five steps away, the literal stuff of nightmares. Caroline focuses on the historian's face, his bristle-brush mustache that twitches as he talks. "Potatoes. Beets. Parsnips, perhaps."

Max laughs. "So you're saying this was a root cellar."

"Perhaps." Favell shifts his weight, purses his lips. "Some information is incomplete."

"What's behind that door?" Caroline asks, surprised at how easy her voice sounds.

"I have it here," Favell says. He rummages in his briefcase for a moment, and then presents a rolled blueprint. He asks Max to hold it up against the concrete block wall, and then runs his finger across it until he finds the mailroom, and then the tunnels.

Caroline steps closer and reads the handwritten text aloud: "Swimming pool?" The question mark is part of the notation.

"Ah, yes," the historian says. The mustache twitches. "In the

1950s, the administration first began considering turning the school into a four-year college for both men and women. As you undoubtedly know," he said, nodding first at Caroline and then at Max, "Bradford did not become a co-educational facility until 1971. However, as I have already mentioned, there was talk of transformation two decades earlier. At that time, plans were developed to install an underground swimming pool. Just here, behind that door."

"An underground swimming pool," Max repeats. He hands the blueprint back to Favell and digs out his notebook. "Could be a good storyline, right?" he says quietly to Caroline, who nods. Max writes screenplays in his spare time, along with half the cast and crew.

"How far did they get in building it?" Caroline asks.

The historian picks through the keys until he finds the one he's looking for. It slides easily into the hole beneath the dead angel doorknob, and Caroline hears Max inhale sharply beside her. She bites the sore spot on her lip and tries to think of the heat of the wine in her belly, the sound of Dan's laughter, the coolness of his skin as they lay in bed in the morning, shoulder to shoulder. The sunlight through the window, the smell of coffee brewing downstairs, the promise of—

There is a high-pitched scream, and then Max shouts, "Jesus Christ!"

"My good man, are you all right?" Favell says, and Caroline laughs. Max is bent over with his hands on his knees, breathing heavily.

"What the hell!" Max says. "Why did you scream?"

"I didn't scream," Caroline replies.

"Not you. Him."

In the dim light, Caroline sees the historian blush. "I was startled," he says. Twitch, twitch.

"It's a concrete wall," Max says.

"I see that now," Favell says. "Please excuse me. I just… I thought I saw something. Right as the door opened."

But there is nothing to see, nothing but a concrete wall. Solid, impenetrable. Caroline takes the camera from Max and snaps a picture, then two. She makes sure that the historian is in one of the shots. Dan will love this story, and photographic evidence will make the telling of it even better.

Favell prattles on about parsnips and the benefits of

co-educational higher learning as he re-locks the door to nothing.
The two men cross the narrow room to the green door, the historian
fussing with his flickering flashlight, Max shoving his notebook into
his pocket and shaking his head.

Caroline faces the door, her shoulders square. She waits a
moment, waits for the panic, waits for the terror to loosen her
bladder, but it does not come. There is nothing behind the door.
Concrete, thick and solid as a tombstone. She closes her eyes and
sees not the door but her father, Jack Winter, flesh over bones, the
face of the wraith at the end of the bed. That dream will still come.

The men are in the mailroom now, their voices muffled. Caroline
opens her eyes, steps to the door, and raises her clenched fist. As
her knuckles touch the splintered wood, something knocks from the
other side, three times fast.

# The Awakening

Six weeks. Gone. A month and a half. Forty-two days. No, correction: Thirty-eight days according to the sour-faced doctor with the silver clipboard and starched collar. Thirty-eight days missing. Gone.

At first there had been sounds: a television, the beeping of machines, the squeak of a wheel in the hallway. Then, light. Painting Isabelle's eyelids with colors: red, yellow, white.

Ceiling. Tile. Her hand, bruised and swollen, a needle pumping her full of… something. Clear liquid dripping into a plastic tube.

Of course she hadn't known she'd lost six weeks when she first woke. It could only have been hours—at most a day—since she collapsed in the church basement. Had her casserole dish shattered? No, Corelle was unbreakable. Beef stroganoff in a white Corelle dish.

Isabelle found the call button and pushed. The ache from the needle travelled up her arm. Withered. Weak.

"Mrs. Richmond?"

A face, round, smiling, came into focus. Isabelle blinked. "Yes?"

"Welcome back."

"Back."

"I'll get the doctor."

This same doctor, at the foot of her bed on the third day since the awakening. Sourpuss expression and polished shoes. Rodriguez. Velasquez. He tapped his silver pen against the silver clipboard, pursed his lips into a knot.

"Your progress is not what I'd expect."

Isabelle smoothed the sheet across her lap. Her mind was weak, unfocused. Mush. Pudding. Chocolate pudding.

Not chocolate. They'd offered her chocolate pudding the first afternoon. Bitter, foul. Thick in her throat. How she'd loved chocolate before—a dark chocolate bar every night after supper, hot chocolate on winter afternoons, thick curls of white chocolate melting on a freshly baked cake, foil-wrapped kisses at the bottom of her purse. Now, bitter. Foul.

Her brain was butterscotch pudding. Tapioca. John's favorite. Or Danielle's.

Day four. "I'm going to increase your physical therapy," Dr. Rodriguez said. He made a note on the chart. "I want you walking by Friday."

Friday, what was Friday?

"You can show your daughter how well you're doing."

Danielle. And her husband. Her husband.

"All right," Isabelle said, and closed her eyes. She listened for the sound of Dr. Rodriguez's shoes, rubber on linoleum. The door whooshed shut behind him.

On the wheeled table next to the bed was a plastic cup of water, a vase of wilted pink and yellow carnations, a stack of get well cards. She'd read them on day two of the awakening, holding them inches from her nose. Glasses lost, forgotten. Cards from friends and neighbors, the church, nieces and nephews and cousins twice-removed.

In the middle of the stack was the wedding invitation. Light blue, embossed silver script.

The date on the invitation: October 18, 2008. A Saturday. Four-thirty p.m. at Our Lady of Grace. Reception at seven at the Moose Lodge. October 18. Ten days ago.

Danielle called on the first night of the awakening, but Isabelle had been too tired to say more than a few words. Exhausted. Eating, yes. Spirits good. Getting better.

On day three they'd talked at length. John's winning touchdown at homecoming, hurricane in Florida, Mr. Potter's heart attack. Everything but the wedding.

On Wednesday, day six, the nurse hung a cartoon picture of a black cat on the wall.

"Happy Halloween," she said. A plastic witch's cauldron dangled from her wrist. "Would you like some candy?"

Full of chocolate. "No, thank you."

"The children will be by on Friday morning." A pumpkin on the wall now. Frankenstein's monster. A vampire.

"For what?"

"Trick or treating." The nurse opened the blinds. Rain splattered against the glass. The black bark of a tree against the gray sky. Crows.

"I don't have anything to give them."

The nurse patted Isabelle's hand. The bruises from the IV had faded. Yellow and green. "I'll find something."

John called. "I won the game, Mom," he said.

"I'm sorry I missed it."

"Me too. Collin passed the ball to Jake, and then—it was wild, Mom, you wouldn't have believed—I was there and I hardly believed it—he threw a lateral—I was on the thirty-yard line, no one was near me! Nobody. I just cruised right in, scored, and we won the game. On homecoming!"

She twisted the phone cord. "That's nice."

"Nice? Mom, it was freakin' sweet! Dad would have loved it, he would have been out of his mind."

Dad. Husband. Isabelle closed her eyes. Dark hair, blue eyes. High forehead, pointed chin. John, a smaller version of Dad. Eyes a darker blue.

John confessed to skipping church, promised to go on Sunday. Couldn't wait to see her. Thanksgiving less than a month away. She would be home by then, home in her own house. He might bring Collin with, if that was okay.

Of course it was. Collin. No face for Collin.

It rained again on Thursday. She spent two hours in Physical Therapy, trying to walk. Learning. Her legs wobbled, feet ached. Sweat in her eyes.

Back in bed, she watched the rain and willed her pudding brain to work. Her husband's birthday: nothing. The name of the cat she'd had as a little girl: Tilly. She hated the taste of things she loved: cabbage and applesauce and chocolate pudding.

Her best friend called from Phoenix. Isabelle tried to picture Helen's face. A blur. They talked about everything but the wedding. She didn't want to ask, but she wanted to know.

On Thursday evening, Dr. Rodriguez came by with his clipboard. "Mrs. Richmond, I'm very pleased with the results of your latest scan." He shined a light into her right eye, then her left. "I think we can talk about getting you home. I'll send Nurse Walker by to discuss the aide schedule."

Friday morning. Halloween. A sky so blue it hurt her eyes. Children on the leaf-strewn street, plastic masks hiding their faces. A jack-o-lantern on the wrought-iron bench in front of Henderson's Drugs. The pharmacist was Patricia Kenniston.

The boys and girls from the children's wing arrived at ten. Isabelle handed out miniature Three Musketeers and Milky Ways to Cinderella, Spider-Man, three tiny doctors, twin witches, and a very small boy wrapped head-to-toe with gauze.

"I'm a mummy," he said.

Lunch was meatloaf, mashed potatoes with gravy, peas. Sitting with her mother at the kitchen table, shelling peas into a big white bowl. Piles of pea husks in paper bags between their feet. Her mother's voice, off-key, singing "The Old Rugged Cross." Smooth wood floor under young Isabelle's bare feet, the ticking of the grandfather clock from the living room, rolling sweet, fresh peas across her tongue. And now, the taste of peas was the taste of rot.

She spit them into the napkin.

Danielle arrived at 4:30. Nick stood in the doorway, his head down. Bright silver band on his finger.

"Oh, Mom, you look great!" Danielle touched Isabelle's hair, tied back with an orange scarf. "You've got the holiday spirit."

"The nurse put it on." Isabelle looked at Nick. "You can come in. Son."

Danielle reached for him. The rings made a tinkling sound when they clasped hands.

Danielle dug into her purse and pulled out a thick envelope. "I brought pictures," she said. "Just some proofs."

The stack of photos was in Isabelle's lap. She blinked to clear her vision. Danielle in white, Nick in a tuxedo, flowers, a limo. A little boy carrying a satin pillow.

"Who is that?"

"Mom, that's Matty. Your grandson."

"Right, yes, I know." She shuffled through the rest of the images, leaving a thumbprint on Nick's mother's face. Her brain knew Nick's mother, Yvonne. She lived in Derry, New Hampshire, and liked to play euchre. Her brain did not know her own grandson. Matty.

Nick walked over to the window and pushed it open. The laughter of children. The honk of a horn. Nick's narrow shoulders and dark hair reminded her of Richard. That was her husband, Richard. He had died in. In. 1992.

Danielle squeezed her hand. Only one bruise now, a pale yellow blossom on her wrinkled skin.

"Mom, we didn't think you were going to wake up."

"But you didn't know."

"You're right. But the lodge was booked. The band. The food."

"But you didn't know."

Nick sighed. "Tell her," he said.

"Tell me what?"

"It doesn't matter," Danielle said. She dug into her purse again. "Look, I brought you something." A blue box, tied with a thin white ribbon.

"Tell me what?"

Danielle opened the box herself. A broach, a cluster of roses. Gold. Or silver. Copper?

"You almost died," Nick said, his voice very loud. "Twice." He kept his back to them, his face turned to the glass. "We drove all night. Sat by your bed. Danielle lost ten pounds."

Isabelle looked at Danielle. Gaunt. Tired. In the wedding photos her cheeks had been full of color, eyes bright.

"We sat and waited for you to die. Should we pull the plug? How long was too long to wait? You weren't breathing on your own. Once, your heart stopped beating. Danielle wanted—"

"Don't," Danielle said. She hung her head, her face hidden behind her hair.

"Danielle wanted to let you go. But John didn't." Nick turned around. "And here you are."

"Here I am."

Danielle pinned the broach to Isabelle's sweater. Isabelle shooed her hands away.

"I'm tired," Isabelle said. "You should go." She closed her eyes and wondered if she was tired. Hungry? Sad.

"Mom, please don't be angry. The doctor said you weren't going to make it. John knew, though, he had faith and I didn't and I'll never forgive myself." Danielle threw herself on Isabelle's knees. Her sobbing shook the bed. "I should have postponed the wedding, I should have, I should have."

Wedding. Honeymoon. Where had she and Richard gone on their honeymoon? Niagara Falls. P. Puh, puh, Poconos. Did she call him Dick? Her fourth grade teacher was Mrs. Barbara Giles. Dick, definitely Dick.

"I'm very tired," Isabelle said.

Nick picked Danielle up off the bed and steered her toward the door. "We'll be back in the morning," he said. He met Isabelle's eyes for the first time. "I'm sorry."

The door shut with a low thunk. Isabelle pulled the wheeled table close. She poked at the peas. Sipped warm milk through a straw. The moon had come out, a fingernail moon hidden in the thick branches of the tree outside the window. Laughter. Ghostly moans. The howl of a werewolf.

When she was six, Danielle had dressed as a pirate. John, only two, a hobo. Red bandana on a stick.

Isabelle took a Milky Way from her pocket and placed it on her tongue. Closed her eyes. Willed herself to like it. To remember. Chocolate.

# Jam

Agnes was wakened from the nap she hadn't meant to take by the sound of breaking glass. She'd fallen asleep on the patio with the gardening trowel in her hand and soil underneath her fingernails. She'd only meant to rest a bit on the patio, then clean herself up and start the roast for dinner. Now the crickets were beginning their night song.

She knew straight away the breaking glass was the jars of strawberry jam being knocked off the counter next to the sink. She had spent the entire morning cooking the jam, pouring it into the quilted crystal jars, and sealing the jars with wax. She had burned the tip of her ring finger on that wax. Now it seemed as if the cat had spoiled her morning's work.

She heard a muffled sound, a human sound, a grunt. The plastic Japanese lanterns strung around the perimeter of the patio flicked on and then off again, and then the lights in the kitchen came on. A perfect square of yellow light illuminated Agnes' feet.

She had slept through the sunset and it was approaching full dark; she ought to be frightened by the thought of someone rummaging around in her kitchen, knocking about her preserves, but she found herself angry instead. Her cheeks flushed; her fists clenched. She pulled herself into a sitting position on the lounge chair and straightened her house coat, which was damp and translucent with sweat.

The kitchen windows were open. Through them came the sound of more breaking—this time the porcelain plate her father had brought home from Denmark. It sat on a brass stand on the butcher block. She dusted it every Saturday morning, the tiny blue figures pulling the sled through the field, the church steeple blanketed in snow. Her father had given that plate to her mother in 1938.

Agnes slipped off her rubber gardening clogs. She grasped the window ledge and pulled herself up to peer inside, her toes gripping the gritty edge of the patio baseboard. If the thief had been looking in the right direction, he would have seen the top of Agnes' head, her hair in a neat braid that hung down to the middle of her back, her eyes narrowed and flashing behind her tinted glasses.

But the thief, quite tall and broad shouldered, was busy violating the drawer of Agnes' great-grandmother's desk in the nook next to the double oven. He rifled through her tax forms and social security check stubs, brushed aside a jumble of linked-together paper clips, and slipped Agnes' father's Swiss Army knife into the front pocket of his trousers.

Agnes' toes and fingers were numb. She lowered herself down from the window and pressed her back against the siding of the house. The only phone was in the kitchen, on the top of the very desk through which the thief was pawing. Her nearest neighbors, the Clarks, were out for a movie and an ice cream cone, their usual Saturday summer evening treat, and they never left their doors unlocked. Agnes would have to confront the thief herself.

As she took several deep, settling breaths, she heard the thief moving from the kitchen into the living room. Agnes moved the glass-topped table with the clay pitcher of gladiolus on it aside so she could stand directly beneath the living room window. The thief had found the television remote; she listened as he changed channels rapidly, finally settling on the station that played country music videos.

"Dude," he said. Agnes stiffened. "I'm at that house out on 54, you should come out." There was a pause, filled with steel guitar. Then: "Nah, it's empty. I checked all the rooms. No car in the garage, either. There's just doilies and shit."

Agnes gritted her teeth. She did not abide cursing. After she confronted the thief with her father's pistol, and made him clean up the shattered glass and strawberry jam, she would slap his filthy mouth. Then she would call the police.

"Bring some beer, man," the thief said. "And this is gonna sound weird, but go to Morgan's and get some of that crusty bread, from the bakery." Another pause and then: "Just get it!"

Agnes heard the thief move back into the kitchen. He would be busy for some time, rummaging through her refrigerator, taking hot dog buns out of the freezer, squeezing her oranges. She hitched up the skirt of her house coat and slipped around the corner of the house.

She had lived in the house since 1973, when she bought it from the Christensens. She'd had the roof redone, filled in the swimming pool, planted rosebushes under the front windows. She'd paid off the mortgage after fourteen years. She'd had the gravel driveway converted to black top, and every Halloween she hung tissue-paper ghosts from the branches of the crab apple tree in the front yard.

The hot water heater went in 1985, and just two years ago the furnace blew its last breath of hot air. Eggs had been tossed at her front door, and once a bag of dog feces, set alight, had been deposited on her front step. But never had anyone breached her home. She did not allow vacuum-cleaner salesmen or Jehovah's Witnesses to cross the threshold. Pastor Jensen knew to pass on his well-wishes to Agnes from the other side of the screen door. Plumbers and electricians entered and exited through the bulkhead basement doors, and if they had to visit the living quarters, Agnes hovered at their elbows and swiped every surface with disinfectant the moment they were gone.

Now a thief, a young man with greased hair and wearing only an undershirt, was inside, spreading his sweat and stink all over Agnes' home. And he had telephoned his friend to help him desecrate her home, to sit on her loveseat and eat her leftover tuna casserole.

At the side of the house, beneath the bedroom window, was the set of slanted bulkhead doors, painted green, that led into the basement. Agnes did not remember locking the doors from the inside; in fact, she could not remember so much as looking at those doors since late April, when the men had come in to replace the basement carpet. With any luck, her atypical lack of attention to detail would be of benefit to her tonight.

She slid her fingers under the right-side handle and pulled. The door protested for a moment and then lifted open with a great, creaking groan. Rust flakes floated down onto the concrete steps. Agnes held the door and her breath. The bulkhead was on the opposite side of the house from the kitchen, and the television was still blaring, so it was unlikely the thief had heard. Still, Agnes' heart beat rapidly for several minutes. When she was confident that she hadn't been heard, she shuffled her way down the steps and through the door into her darkened basement.

Agnes moved quickly across the floor of the main room, filled with several chairs, a coffee table, and a black and white television that received three channels. She passed the laundry room, fragrant with lilac-scented dryer sheets and bleach, and moved into the cool dark of the office. Her rubber shoes squeaked on the cement floor.

In the far corner of the room, behind the plastic-encased stack of *Life* magazines, was the safe. The hulking gray mass had been delivered from her parents' house when Agnes had bought the Christensen home in 1973. She rarely looked inside; besides a copy of her mother's will and Agnes' own Social Security card, the only thing inside was the gun. She had fired it once, over a decade ago, sending a bullet into the side of a bale of hay in the field behind the house. The gun had felt greasy and unnatural in her grip.

Muffled voices carried down to her: The thief's friend had arrived. The basement office was directly beneath the kitchen; Agnes listened closely, her fingers twitching against the dial of the safe. The intruders stomped back and forth across the kitchen floor, opening and slamming shut cupboard doors. The microwave oven timer dinged, and the thief and his friend laughed.

16-9-24. The safe clicked open. The gun was wrapped in a soft tan cloth. A small box of bullets had been shoved to the back of the safe, but Agnes did not reach for it. She always kept the gun loaded. She put it into the pocket of her dressing gown, which caused the flimsy cotton to sag. She closed the safe and spun the dial of the lock; she didn't need the thief and his friend stealing her important papers as well as her food.

Leaving her shoes at the bottom of the stairs, she walked quickly but silently up to the door. It was, as always, open several inches in order to allow the cat to access his litter box down in the laundry room. Agnes recalled letting the cat out after lunch, so she at least did not have to fear that the thief or his friend would harm him.

"Dude, this shit is sick!"

This was a new voice, the voice of the thief's friend, higher-pitched and less confident sounding. Still the same foul mouth.

"This is better than any of that shit you get at a store," the thief said.

Agnes sniffed. They were eating her jam. Her strawberry jam. The jam for which she had harvested the berries herself, from Tomion's U-Pick on Fergusons Corners Road, coming home each morning stiff, her fingers stained deep pink with berry juice and the cuffs of her trousers wet with dew. She had hulled each berry, had rinsed each one gently before chopping the lot to meaty bits. She had stood over the stove in the heat of the late June morning, pouring in the heaped cups of sugar, stirring the mixture until it bubbled, adding the pectin. She had skimmed the pink foam from the top of the roiling mix, collecting it in a porcelain tea cup that had belonged to her great-grandmother. Later, after the jam was cooling in crystal jars on the counter next to the sink, she'd spread the skimmed foam onto a slice of white bread for her dinner.

"Whose house is this?" the thief's friend asked, his mouth thick with Agnes' jam.

"That old bitch I told you about. I followed her home from the drug store last week? She had a shitload of stuff in her cart. Like three boxes of Sudafed."

"Bullshit. You can't buy more than one box at a time."

"No, this was at Henderson's, they know her. She asked for three boxes and they gave it to her, no questions."

"Where's she keep it?"

"Probably in the bathroom. Give me that." Agnes heard the familiar tinkling of knife against glass. "You ate it all? Dick."

They had finished an entire jar of her jam. Jam that she used as gifts for her neighbors, for Pastor Jensen, for the young postal worker who delivered her seed catalogs and the occasional letter from her niece in Scranton. And she always saved two jars to get her through the winter, to spread on browned English muffins in the dark of a January morning. The thief had broken what sounded like several jars when he first entered her home, and now he and his friend had eaten another.

Agnes felt the weight of the gun against her thigh. She pushed the door with the tips of her fingers and stepped around the corner.

The kitchen table was filthy with bread crumbs, jam-slick knives, and puddles of spilled milk. A case of beer, its cardboard topped ripped open, was on the butcher block next to the napkin holder, along with a set of car keys and a package of cigarettes. The microwave was open, emitting a stench of burned cheese. Hanging from the back of one of the chairs was a denim jacket. Sticking out of the jacket pocket was a battered leather wallet.

Agnes placed the wallet in the empty pocket of her house coat before moving slowly through the kitchen to the narrow hallway that led to the living room, the bathroom, and her bedroom beyond. The television blared a song by Johnny Cash, one she recognized, about a ring of fire. Agnes clenched her fist until she felt her fingernails bite into the soft flesh of her palm.

"Dude, in here."

The thief was in her bedroom. Agnes stole a glance down the hallway from her position in the living room. The thief's friend, hair long and tied at his neck with a hank of rawhide, jogged the few steps from the bathroom to the bedroom, his dirty sneakers slapping against the hardwood floor.

Agnes followed.

"Found it," the thief said. He pointed to a stack of red and white cardboard boxes on Agnes' night stand. "Three boxes. I told you." He tossed one of the boxes across the room. His friend fumbled a moment and then caught it. "I'm gonna sell these to Chuck."

"I don't know, man. I think we should just go," the friend said.

The thief laughed. "You're such a pussy."

"Let's just take it and go, then," the friend said. His voice was hardly more than a whisper. Agnes moved closer to the door.

"No way, man. *Die Hard's* on later. I'm gonna order a pizza."

The friend sighed and sat down on the bed, wrinkling the comforter, and that's when Agnes stepped into the room. She fumbled for a moment with the gun as the hammer caught on the fabric of her house coat pocket, but then it was steady in her hand. She rested her pointer finger against the trigger.

"Hands up," she said. Her voice was firm.

The thief dropped the other two boxes of sinus medication on the floor. "Huh," he said in a rush of breath, as if he had been kicked in the stomach. The thief's friend turned around slowly until he was facing Agnes. His cheeks and forehead were alive with red blemishes, but all other color had drained from his face. He was barely seventeen.

"Run!" he shouted, his voice cracking. Agnes and the thief watched as the boy dashed to the open window and threw himself through the screen. Agnes winced at the sound of her hydrangeas being trampled.

"Young man," she said, leveling the gun at the thief, "please follow me."

"Listen, lady, I don't—"

Agnes waggled the gun. "Just move."

They walked down the hall together, the thief in front, Agnes in back, the gun between them. When they reached the kitchen, Agnes used the barrel of the gun to prod the thief toward the sink.

"I want you to clean that mess up," Agnes said.

"What mess?" the thief said, even as glass crunched beneath his stained shoes.

"You spoiled my jam."

"That's good jam, lady."

"What did you say?" Agnes used the gun to usher the man into a chair. He sat down.

"That's the best jam I've had since I was a kid." The thief smiled. His teeth were white and straight. "My grandma used to make it just like that."

Agnes stood over him, the barrel of the gun pointed at his chest. "If you had a grandmother who cared enough for you to make you strawberry jam, then you should know better than to break into someone's home."

The thief frowned. "She's dead."

"I'm sorry to hear that."

The thief shook his head and started to stand up, but Agnes poked him with the gun. The grease on the barrel left a circular stain on his undershirt. The thief settled back again. "What's the name of that stuff you use to make it firm up? Looks like clear Jell-o?"

"Pectin."

"Right! Grandma used to let me squeeze that shit out of the package."

"Watch your mouth."

The thief laughed and lunged at Agnes at the same time. She cut her heel on a shard of glass, but maintained her balance.

"Sorry, lady," the thief said, his palms out. He had a yellow rubber bracelet on his wrist. "Sorry. Maybe you can put that gun down, you know?"

"You broke into my home," Agnes said. "You disturbed my papers. You burned a burrito in my microwave."

"Listen," the thief said, and took a step closer. Agnes tightened her grip on the gun. "I'm sorry about the mess. You got a mop? I'll clean it up."

"And you ate my jam," Agnes finished.

"Well, yeah," the thief said. He made a quick movement that Agnes couldn't quite follow, and then thrust his arm forward. "And I took your knife, too." Agnes' hand spasmed and the gun went off.

"Jesus Christ!" the thief shouted. He patted his chest and stomach, but there was no wound. Agnes had shot the coffee maker.

She could no longer stand. She slumped to the floor, her fingers still tight around the gun. Her father's Swiss Army knife, now bloody, was in her lap. Blood bloomed on her dressing gown.

"Stupid bitch," the thief said. He knelt down and breathed beer and burrito stench into Agnes' face. He had traces of mustache on his upper lip, fine blonde hairs. "You make good jelly, though," he said, and then picked up the knife and jabbed it twice more into the soft flesh of her belly.

He stood over her for several minutes, and gradually she let her breathing slow. When he seemed satisfied that she was dead, he picked up the two unbroken jars of jam off the floor and deposited them into the bulky pockets on the sides of his pants. Agnes listened as the thief walked down the hallway to the bedroom and back. When he returned to the kitchen, she opened her eyes just enough to see him cradling the boxes of Sudafed in the crook of his elbow.

He took the remains of the six pack of beer and his keys. He left the screen door open behind him.

After the sound of the thief's engine grew distant, Agnes struggled to a sitting position in the spreading pool of her blood and sugared strawberries. She wrapped her hand around the leg of the butcher block and pulled, her knees crunching on quilted crystal and Danish porcelain. She felt the weight of the thief's wallet in the pocket of her dressing gown as she began the slow ascent to the telephone on her great-grandmother's desk.

# The Widow's Walk

The walk, from the front door to the lighthouse at the end of the cape and back, was just under two miles. Carol put on a faded blue coaching t-shirt of Walt's, "Mustang Pride" in cracked orange lettering on the front, and her comfy elastic-waist white pants—the only pair that didn't pinch around the middle. She'd gained weight since the hip replacement, oh yes.

She hadn't worn any kind of exercise shoe in ages. They were stiff and heavy on her feet and made her pinky toes tingle. She stood on the front step, shaking one foot and then the other. When the tingling didn't go away, she grasped her cane firmly in her right hand and struck out for the road.

It was sticky and humid, but overcast. She thought about taking an umbrella, but didn't like the idea of having both hands occupied. If she fell again, she would need one hand free to catch herself. Jack barked at her from the front step as she waddled away up the hill. Walt had walked Jack up to the lighthouse and back twice a day, every day. But taking Jack along meant the poop scooper, a plastic bag, a bottle of water. Too much to worry about.

They first came to the cape forty-three years before, on their one-year anniversary. Walt had just gotten tenure at the high school where he taught Spanish and coached boys' track and field. To celebrate, he booked them in a beachside motel on the southern coast for an entire week. It was a huge extravagance: two hundred dollars, more than their mortgage payment.

"Let's have a toast," he'd said, pouring red wine into plastic cups. "To a whole year as man and wife."

"I shouldn't," Carol said. She sipped at the wine but didn't really drink. She was sure she was pregnant, but she hadn't told Walt yet.

"Tomorrow I want to go see that lighthouse there, at the end
of the cape." They stood on the slanted balcony of the dingy little
room. The sun was setting behind the motel, the beach full of
shadows and seagulls. "There's a road that goes along the edge, see
it there?" He took her hand and pointed in the direction of the gray
ribbon leading out to the little snip of land with the lighthouse on it.
"Looks like three or four miles. Think you can make it?"

"You probably can't keep up with me," she said.

"I had a dream about that."

"What, keeping up with me?"

"That lighthouse." He took her hand in his and said, "I love
you." He said the words often, but they still made her heart race.

They woke early the next morning. Carol wore the floppy straw
hat she used when she gardened to keep the sun out of her eyes.
The road was new; the bottoms of their shoes were soon gummed
with fresh tar. There was ocean to their right, foamy and blue, new
houses to their left, cozy capes and ranches with green or blue siding
and black shutters. Bicycles were abandoned in driveways; white
undershirts fluttered from backyard clotheslines. Like houses in any
small town—if your front yard was a ragged cliff leading
down to the glittering, huge, impossible ocean. Walt's eyes never

left the lighthouse.

The cape road rose gradually as it stretched out into the Atlantic, then dropped, sloping the final quarter mile to a little parking area beside the lighthouse and a grassy spot with a half dozen or so picnic tables. At the very top of the hill, just before the road began to drop back down to sea level, was a new house: a brick mansion, massive and dark, rising out of the rocky land.

"That's too bad," Walt said, his hands on his hips.

Carol bent to tie her shoe. "What is?"

"That house. It's going to block the ocean view for everyone on the other side of the road." He looked over at the freshly painted sign advertising lots for sale and sighed.

She loved everything about the house: the impeccable landscaping, the soaring peaks, the gleaming windows. She felt color burn in her cheeks. Walt's face looked old and sad.

Forty years later, the brick house was among the smallest on the cape. Small and unassuming now, from Carol's vantage point on the road. Still almost a mile away.

She planted her right foot and then lurched forward, trying not to lean so heavily on the cane. Walt's plastic pedometer, clipped to the waistband of her pants, said she'd gone 450 steps. A little river of sweat had formed between her breasts and another was running between her shoulder blades. If Walt could see her now.

They had moved to the cape ten years ago, the year Walt retired. After years of scrimping and saving and searching, he'd finally found a house on the cape they could afford. In the evenings, while she stirred spaghetti sauce and Jack sat obediently at her feet, Walt showed her pictures of the little white house, two stories with a peaked roof and a tiny widow's walk. A brass rooster weathervane. A one-car garage. He promised her they'd be able to see the ocean. And they could—from the widow's walk.

It was hugely beyond their means. One of the smallest houses on the cape, it was still close to half a million dollars. They'd lived well in their little upstate town, had paid for their daughter's schooling, had owned their house and both cars. But on the cape they were in debt again. They would have to work.

Ellen had been furious about the move. "But Mom, you love it here. You love your house!"

"I love the coast more," Carol had said, and tried her best to believe it.

She did love it, there was no lie in that. And even though she resented having to work again, having to find a job (which took the better part of that first summer), having to acclimate herself to a new town, a new grocery store, a new pharmacist, new doctors, she loved the water and the wind, the sailboats cutting through the foam, the sunrise that turned the water blood red, butter yellow. She loved the color in Walt's cheeks when he and Jack got home from their morning walk, sweeping in the front door with the smell of fresh air and sunlight trailing behind.

By the time Carol reached the crest of the hill, she had a stitch in her side and her lungs burned. She rubbed at her new hip, which ached just walking across the living room to change the television station. Not so "new," really, as the fall that had taken away most of her independence and all of her coffee shop job had happened more than eight months ago.

She looked up at the brick mansion that she had first seen, and envied, when she was a newlywed. The begonias on the porch were wilted and the morning paper was still in the driveway.

"Hello there, Mrs. Davis."

"Hello, Greg."

Greg had moved into the brick mansion just two months before Walt died. She had brought the young man a tuna casserole and a loaf of applesauce bread. Walt had helped him fix his lawn mower and told him the best place to get pancakes. Greg was alone in the big house; his wife and children were in California for reasons Carol could not remember.

"How are things? All right?" The lights and siren from the ambulance had woken Greg as well as the rest of the neighbors that early morning two weeks ago. They came out on their porches and stood with their arms crossed as the paramedics took Walt away.

"I'm going for a walk."

"How's your hip?"

"Better."

"Where you going? I'll walk with you for a bit, if you don't mind."

"Down to the lighthouse."

Greg was thin and pale and always looked like he needed a nap. His brown hair stuck to his pink scalp in wisps. He was like a reed, long and brittle, whereas Walt had been solid and strong, legs like the trunks of old trees.

Greg stepped in beside her, and they walked to the sound of the gulls overhead and their shoes against the pavement. It was all downhill, which should have been easier but was harder. Carol's hip began to ache, and the calf of her left leg cramped up. She tried to control her breathing, but Greg heard her pant.

"Let's slow down, Mrs. Davis." He took her by the elbow and led her to the side of the road. She put her hand on a fancy iron mailbox. "Maybe you're going too far too fast."

"Walter used to walk Jack down here and back every day."

Greg knew; Greg had started walking with Walt and Jack in the mornings. He hadn't been there on *the* morning, though. No, Greg had slept in that day. Would it have made a difference?

"I just want to get down to the lighthouse," Carol said. No one could have helped Walt. The doctor said his heart practically exploded, the heart attack was so great.

Greg sighed and stuck his hands deep into the pockets of his pants. "How about this? We'll walk down there together and then I'll run back up and get the car. How's that?"

Carol looked up at him, his sunken eyes and freckled cheeks, and said, "That'll do."

It took half an hour to get down the hill, with frequent stops for Carol to catch her breath or rub her hip or stretch her calf. Finally they were there, the lighthouse was right in front of her, Walt's precious lighthouse.

It had stood on the end of the cape for almost two hundred years, keeping watch, guiding sailors safely into the bay. The light swept across Carol and Walt's bedroom, flashes of white light invading her sleep, night after night.

She closed the curtains after Walt died, so she could sleep without the lighthouse watching her. The lighthouse that had called to Walt for half his life, that had brought them here, that had witnessed his collapse and death. That stood sentry over her empty house. She refused to look at it, to give it the satisfaction of her acknowledgement. He had collapsed at its feet, Jack barking at the sky and nudging Walt's arm with his wet nose.

"There she is," said Greg.

Carol raised her eyes. She opened her hand and let the cane fall to the gravel. A strong breeze raised gooseflesh on her bare arms.

"I'll go get the car."

She looked up at the lighthouse and the lighthouse looked down at her, silent and steady. She turned her face to the sky and smelled the open water and felt her heart break and then, in an instant, mend again.

# Thank yous

This collection wouldn't exsist without the keen eye and kind attention of Johanna Lester, Namer of All Things. I couldn't live my best life without you, Jojo.

To my Bobs, Kim Dowd and Heather Spencer, for being attentive and enthusiastic listeners (and my favorite backup singers).

To E. Christopher Clark, who helped me earn my first dollars as a fiction writer. And to the gone-but-never-forgotten Bradford College for bringing us together. Surgo ut prosim.

To the faces and places of Penn Yan that fill up so many of these pages. Home is where my story begins.

To my support staff: Sarah Wedge-Merrill, Lisa Wesneski, Leah Flynn Gallant, Mandy Chalou, Leigh Anna Thompson, Laurie Ritt, the FHCB, Tammy Hines, Rebecca Dudek, Paula McKenna, and Brenda Snyder Penner. Y'all are the proverbial wind beneath my wings. Thanks for keeping me afloat.

To Mom and Dad and Jennie for all the rest.

Made in the USA
Middletown, DE
27 October 2015